CRITICAL ACCLAIM FOR

Catherine Aird

'Catherine Aird is as clever a detective writer as Margery Allingham.' *Times Literary Supplement*

'The doyenne of the British whodunnit spins an engrossing riddle.' *Peterborough Evening Telegraph*

'Carefully and originally plotted, elegantly and amusingly written . . . light, ingenious and a pleasure to read.' *Times Literary Supplement*

'There is a delightful, slightly naughty flavour about this sly, wittily observant and wholly delicious confection by the much admired Catherine Aird.' *Hampstead and Highgate Express*

'Aird's delicious concoctions are never less than elegant and mischievously sharp; she manipulates her often bizarre plots and people with confidence.' *The Times*

'Light-hearted and told with a playful wit and elegance that is quite captivating.' *Birmingham Post*

'Gorgeously entertaining.' *Daily Telegraph*

'A shining star . . . a most ingenious lady.'
The New Yorker

'An amusingly written whodunnit with an original plot.' *Herald Express*

Stiff News

Catherine Aird served as Chairman of the Crime Writers' Association from 1990 to 1991 and is the author of some eighteen crime novels, the most recent of which, *Little Knell*, is now available in Macmillan hardback. She has also written a *son et lumière* and has edited a number of parish histories. In recognition of her work she was awarded an honorary MA from the University of Kent and was made an MBE for her services to the Girl Guide Association.

In October 1992 she was the first recipient of the CWA/Hertfordshire Libraries Golden Handcuffs Award for her outstanding contribution to detective fiction.

Though she has lived in East Kent for many years, she was brought up in Huddersfield.

By the same author

Catherine Aird

Stiff News

PAN BOOKS

First published 1998 by Macmillan

This edition published 2000 by Pan Books
an imprint of Macmillan Publishers Ltd
25 Eccleston Place, London SW1W 9NF
Basingstoke and Oxford
Associated companies throughout the world
www.macmillan.co.uk

ISBN 0 330 37026 X

1 3 5 7 9 8 6 4 2

A CIP catalogue record for this book is available from
the British Library.

Phototypeset by Intype London Ltd
Printed and bound in Great Britain by
Mackays of Chatham plc, Chatham, Kent

The chapter headings are taken from 'Death the Leveller'
by James Shirley (1596–1666).

For David Barton with love

Messenger: Labienus –
This is stiff news – hath, with his Parthian force,
Extended Asia from Euphrates;
His conquering banner shook from Syria
To Lydia and to Ionia

Antony and Cleopatra, Act I Sc. ii

Chapter One

The glories of our blood and state

'No,' said Mrs Maisie Carruthers somewhat breathlessly. She was lying propped up in a hospital bed looking very frail, a tiny little figure amidst the pillows. 'Never.'

'But Mummy . . .' Ned Carruthers still called his mother that largely because he had lacked the courage to change when change had been possible. Now his mother objected to change of any sort.

Which was part of the trouble today.

'No,' said Mrs Carruthers again. She started drumming her hands on the sheets.

'But Mummy, the doctor says . . .'

Mrs Carruthers had lived too long to be overly concerned with medical opinion. 'The doctor said I wouldn't lived more than a year.'

'That was when you were a baby,' responded Ned patiently, having heard this tale many times before. 'Things were different then. Now, Mummy, the ward sister suggests that . . .'

'No,' said Mrs Carruthers rather less breathlessly.

'The doctor says,' repeated Ned, reverting to the higher medical authority and trying hard to think of his mother as a particularly difficult and recalcitrant client and treat her accordingly, 'that you're not fit to go home and live there alone any longer.'

'He can't stop me.' Mrs Carruthers folded her matchstick arms across her chest in an attitude that the behavioural psychologists had good reason to deem aggressive.

Ned sighed.

'And neither can you,' remarked Mrs Carruthers belligerently.

It was significant that Ned Carruthers was not looking at his mother but was instead staring out of the window of the ward. He was a landscape architect by profession and had in his mind's eye already redesigned for the better the singularly unattractive hospital grounds. Wouldn't the powers that be ever understand that the sight of a decent garden induced as much healing as did their precious pills and potions?

'No, Mummy,' agreed Ned absently. In his mother's case it hadn't been pills and potions that she had needed but an operation. It had been an accident – a fall, actually – that had taken her into hospital, the classic 'old lady's accident' that had resulted in the broken neck of a femur. Now she'd got a spanking new hip and they'd said she could go on for years.

But not at home.

Alone.

'I'll just die in here instead,' said Mrs Carruthers, at the same moment as, in his mind, Ned had grubbed out those ghastly yew trees – a reminder of a churchyard if ever there was one – and mentally moved a barely tolerable flower bed. He continued his train of thought, in imagination restocking the flower bed with low-maintenance, sweet-scented flowering shrubs and resiting it over by the rustic garden bench presented in memory of a former – and late – patient.

'Or at home,' his mother added, since he didn't appear to be paying attention.

Ned's wife, Stella, was on record as having said that she didn't think her mother-in-law had any intention of dying in the hospital, at home or anywhere else.

Ever.

'Yes, Mummy,' he said. 'I mean, no.' He took a deep breath and reluctantly abandoned thinking about the desirability of having a pleached hornbeam trellis put in to catch the eye at the far end of the grounds and disguise what looked suspiciously like a mortuary chapel. 'However, as it is, the Manor at Almstone . . .'

'No,' said his mother.

'The Manor at Almstone,' he persisted, 'just happens to have an empty room.'

Maisie Carruthers sat up. 'Who's died?' she asked sharply.

'Someone called Mrs Gertrude Powell,' he said unwillingly, a spasm of genuine pity crossing his face. After all, it couldn't be much fun living on and watching all your friends and contemporaries predecease you. 'Did you know her?'

'Me, know Gertie Powell?' The old lady gave a high cackle. 'Course I did. The Pride of the Regiment, we called her.'

'I'm sorry . . .' he stumbled.

'Catnip to men,' said Mrs Carruthers succinctly.

'I understand that Captain Markyate is a patient there at the Manor, too,' said Ned. Peter Markyate had been a feature of his own childhood in the shadowy role of honorary uncle.

'All gong and no dinner,' said the old lady elliptically.

Ned thought he'd better get back to the matter in hand. 'Because of Mrs Powell having died,' he said, 'they're willing to have you at the Manor as soon as you're ready to leave here.'

This was more than could be said for Stella, who was most definitely not willing to have her mother-in-law to live with them in their house. Ned was hoping that he would be able to avoid having to say this.

'No.'

'Immediately, in fact,' said her son.

'No.'

'You're eligible to go there because of Daddy,' persisted Ned. He had already discussed his

4

mother's position at length with the doctor, the ward sister and the social worker. What he hadn't liked about their discussions was the constant use by the healing professions of the phrase 'disposal of the patient'. It smacked to him rather too much of the phrase 'disposal of the remains'. Glancing down at his mother now he realized that perhaps those three experienced professionals weren't quite so far off the mark as he'd first thought. She was nothing but a bag of bones.

'No,' said Mrs Carruthers again.

A bag of bones with a mind of its own, of course, sighed Ned to himself. And a tongue. He said aloud, 'It's a very nice place. Some people would give their eye teeth to get in there . . .'

The Manor at Almstone – one of the younger Robert Smythson's minor works – had been the ancestral home of a young man killed in 1915 in that fearsome culling of heirs called the Battle of Loos. His sorrowing parents, without other lineal descendants, had left a perfect jewel of a Calleshire Tudor manor house to their son's old Regiment – the Fearnshires – in perpetuity 'for the comfort and welfare of former members of the Regiment and their families for all time . . . the Colonel of the Regiment for the time being and the Regimental Chaplain to be joint trustees'.

'No,' reiterated Mrs Carruthers with spirit.

'Daddy always wanted you to go there,' ventured Ned, although he knew that this could not by any stretch of the imagination be called a trump card. The late Major General Hector Carruthers might have been a fine figure of a man, a force to be reckoned with in regimental affairs and a pillar of society, but it was generally agreed that his remit had never ever run inside his own front door.

'No,' said the major general's widow flatly.

It took the best part of an hour, during which she had conducted a strategic retreat worthy of a five-star general, before Mrs Maisie Carruthers agreed to be admitted to the Manor at Almstone. She had fought every yard of the way, only yielding an inch at a time, before tearfully dismissing her only son as heartless and uncaring. She finally conceded defeat, sinking dramatically back on her pillows, her eyes apparently closed in both mental and physical pain.

Ned Carruthers, wrung dry of every emotion save guilt, bent down and kissed her forehead, brushing aside her wispy white hair to do so. 'Bye-bye, Mummy,' he said, feeling reduced to a frazzle and fit for nothing – and most certainly not for his wife's tart observations. Stella, he knew, would be notably unsympathetic to his exhaustion. 'I'm sure you'll settle down there all right,' he said, sounding unconvincing even to himself.

Mrs Carruthers waited until she heard the ward door close behind him before she opened her eyes again. Making sure that Ned had really and truly gone and that she was now quite alone, she sat up and removed her dentures. Then she sank back on her plumped-up pillows, an expression of great satisfaction on her old face.

From the very beginning she had always had every intention when the time came of ending her days at Almstone Manor. However, she had seen no reason at all for giving in and going there without a struggle.

Now if she found anything there not to her liking it would be well known that she had never wanted to go to the Manor in the first place – even, perhaps, that she had been forced there against her will by her unfeeling family.

Which should make it very much easier for her to leave the place in high dudgeon if things didn't work out the way she wanted.

Most important of all, though, was that before she got to Almstone Manor, Brigadier Hamish MacIver should hear that she hadn't ever wanted to come there in the first place . . .

The morning after she arrived there the gentleman in question was preparing to mount the steps of the great brass lectern in Almstone Church. He had been invited – as befitted his position as one of the most senior residents at the Manor – to give a reading at Mrs Gertude Powell's funeral. Brigadier Hamish MacIver was every inch the retired military man. That is to say he was as spick and span as it was humanly possible for an elderly officer with arthritis but without a batman to be.

He had marched from his pew to the foot of the lectern just as one day long ago he had marched across the parade ground at Sandhurst. He had halted in front of the two carpeted steps and climbed them stiffly now with a care not entirely unassociated with the wearing of bifocal spectacles.

'The reading,' he announced, 'is from the Book of Psalms.' As he straightened the page, he spared a glance for the front pew and still registered an absentee from Gertie Powell's obsequies. It was just as he had thought when he had first cast a look in that direction from his own pew. Gertie's son, Lionel, wasn't there.

He gave a silent sniff. Trust that stiff, acidulous windbag Lionel Powell not to get to the church on time, even for his own mother's funeral. Civil servants were like that, of course. In his own mind, the Brigadier had always equated civil servants with the General Staff. Good on paper; no good at all when it came to action on the front line. Only they would call the front line the 'cutting edge' or something equally meaningless these days ... nothing was the same any more.

Nothing.

'Psalm one hundred and twenty-one,' declared MacIver. He saw, though, that there was a brace of young girls sitting in the front pew reserved for the family mourners. Most probably, decided the

Brigadier, they were Lionel's two daughters – Gertie's granddaughters – and kept from her as much as possible by Lionel and his stuffy wife. What a pity it was, he thought in passing, that the wooden fronts of the pews in this church went all the way down to the floor because one of the girls looked as if she might have good ankles.

Like Gertie.

Hamish MacIver gave a nostalgic sigh, gripped the sides of the lectern firmly, and began to read aloud. 'I will lift up mine eyes unto the hills,' he said, 'from whence cometh my help . . .'

Only the help had never come, not when he had wanted it, two days out of Mersa Matruh in that terrible wadi. All he had seen then when lifting his tired, sand-blown eyes to the hills were enemy tanks. Unbidden as usual, the memory of desert warfare intruded into his thoughts. He strove, as always, to banish the spectre. Cognitive therapy, they called the treatment for shell-shock now. They even called shell-shock something else these days.

Nothing stayed the same any more. Nothing.

'My help cometh from the Lord,' he read, concentrating on the words in front of him. He'd noticed these flashbacks were happening more and more frequently these days. 'Which made heaven and earth.'

Perhaps Lionel Powell hadn't come to the funeral today on purpose – making a last gesture of disapproval towards the mother whom he'd always regarded more than a little censoriously. The Brigadier dismissed this possibility almost at once. Not only, until the service had started, had the front pew's two occupants kept on turning to look expectantly towards the south door but, in his book, Lionel didn't have enough spunk to do something like that.

Not Lionel.

Damn silly name to give a boy . . . Hamish MacIver pulled himself up with a jerk as he remembered why Gertie's son was given the name of Lionel. Only Gertie would have named her son after the most senior officer in the battalion and not her husband. Trust Gertie. She just didn't care. Never had.

'He will not suffer thy foot to be moved,' read on the Brigadier evenly, 'he that keepeth thee will not slumber. Behold, he that keepeth Israel shall neither slumber nor sleep. . .' At least the psalmist knew what he was writing about – that bit might have been written especially for watch-keepers and . . . sentries. Don't even think about sentries, the old soldier adjured himself sternly, and certainly not about a foot that moved. Think about something that didn't matter. Think about whether Miss Ritchie was here in the church today and whether she'd contrived to sit next to old Walter Bryant as usual. No power on earth could keep Miss Ritchie out of a church if she wanted to enter it and well she knew it. There was no ecclesiastical law yet about whom you sat next to in church, either, whatever Walter Bryant's two daughters might have liked.

The Brigadier worked his way through the psalm, conscious that at least as far as Gertie Powell was concerned the reading had been a better choice for the occasion than the anthem. The Rector had chosen the anthem – but then the Rector hadn't really known Gertie. Not in her heyday, anyway. Otherwise he wouldn't ever have had all those innocent-looking choirboys up there singing Purcell's famous anthem 'Thou Knowest Thou, Lord, the Secrets of Our Hearts' while looking as if butter wouldn't melt in their mouths. He, Hamish MacIver, could tell them a thing or two about secrets, all right.

'The Lord is thy keeper,' declaimed the Brigadier in his customary clipped military tones. 'The Lord is thy shade upon thy right hand. The sun shall not smite thee by day, nor the moon by night . . .'

He nearly faltered then. The sun had smitten them all day in the wadi and the moon had brought no comfort at all . . . With a conscious effort of will, Brigadier Hamish MacIver contemplated the two girls – young women really – in the front pew. One of them looked so like her grandmother that he didn't need to see what her ankles were like.

He could guess.

The other girl had more of the look of Lionel's tedious wife, Julia. Lionel's wife's ankles were no good at all – and the rest of her wasn't much better.

And condemnatory with it into the bargain. Not that Gertie had cared about that either.

'The Lord shall preserve thee from all evil.' He tried to read the rest of the psalm automatically and without thinking about the words. He didn't quite succeed. 'He shall preserve thy soul. The Lord shall preserve thy going out and thy coming in . . .' Only He hadn't. Not in the wadi. Not everyone. 'From this time forth, and even for evermore.' MacIver shut the Bible firmly and said, 'Amen'.

'Amen,' said the congregation.

The Brigadier found getting down from the lectern more difficult than getting to it had been. Not only was there his gammy leg but there was his arthritis . . . Matron – Mrs Peden – knew only too well about both disabilities and was watching him from the other side of the church. He could see her out of the corner of his eye looking at him now, as anxious as he was that he didn't fall. He murmured her little aide-mémoire under his breath – the rest of the congregation probably thought he was praying. 'Up with the good, down with the bad,' he chanted to himself, as he carefully sank his weight onto his wounded leg, bringing the good one gratefully down beside it without disaster. He rephrased the mnemonic. 'Good foot first to heaven, bad foot first to hell.' That wasn't such a bad sentiment for reciting in church anyway.

Hamish MacIver straightened his shoulders and marched back to his own seat, resolving that as soon as he decently could he'd make his way over to Matron and find out if she knew why Lionel and Julia Powell weren't there at the funeral. She'd know what had happened to them. Bound to. Matron – like all matrons – made it her business to know that sort of thing. Indeed, Mrs Peden always did know everything – well, very nearly everything.

But even Muriel Peden didn't know where Lionel Powell and his wife were. And at that precise moment only a very few people did.

One of those who did know was Detective Inspector C.D. Sloan of F Division of the Calleshire Constabulary.

This was because Lionel and Julia Powell were at the police station in Berebury.

Chapter Two

Are shadows, not substantial things

'Come in, Sloan, come in,' Superintendent Leeyes was barking through his open door, 'and listen to this, will you?'

'Sir?' Detective Inspector Sloan had just dutifully responded to an urgent summons to the office of his superior. With the Superintendent were a middle-aged couple.

'These are Mr and Mrs Lionel Powell.' The Superintendent waved an arm in the direction of a solemn-looking pair in their early fifties dressed in conspicuously dark clothes. They were sitting together at the other side of the Superintendent's desk. A piece of paper and an opened envelope lay on the desk between the two and the Superintendent. Leeyes said gruffly by way of introduction, 'Inspector Sloan . . .'

Detective Inspector C.D. Sloan, known as Christopher Dennis to his wife and family and – for obvious reasons – to his friends and everyone at the police station as 'Seedy', was the head of the tiny

14

Criminal Investigation Department of Berebury Divison of the Calleshire Constabulary. Such crime as there was in F Division usually found its way onto Sloan's desk rather than the Superintendent's, so this case – if there was a case, that is – didn't fit the usual pattern for a start. He turned enquiringly now towards Leeyes and the two strangers.

'Say it again,' the Superintendent imperiously commanded the man in the dark suit. 'Tell it just like you told me.'

Lionel Powell leaned forward and began. 'My late mother's funeral is arranged for today at twelve noon at St Clement's Church at Almstone.'

Unconsciously Sloan's eyes strayed towards the clock above the Superintendent's head. The hands stood at ten minutes to twelve o'clock.

'My wife and I live at the far side of the county and naturally we started off this morning in good time.' Lionel Powell paused.

'Er – naturally,' agreed Detective Inspector Sloan. Funerals called for punctuality if anything did: undertakers waited for no man.

'On our way out of the gate I met our postman and so I took the letters – all this morning's post, that is – from him and put them in my pocket without opening them.' Lionel Powell gave a little cough. 'Obviously, Inspector, I didn't want to delay leaving home – not in the – er – circumstances.'

'Naturally,' said Sloan again.

'However, as we had left in very good time we

15

got over to East Calleshire early. Much too early.' Powell hesitated. 'You see, we didn't really want to present ourselves at the Manor before the – er – proceedings . . . and our two daughters had arranged to go straight to the church. They were coming independently from London.'

'We were, of course, going back to the Manor after the funeral,' contributed Mrs Julia Powell, sounding as if she hadn't relished the prospect. 'They made it very clear that we were expected there then and that there was no need for us to do anything ourselves . . .'

Her husband said swiftly, 'We were assured, Inspector, that it has always been the custom of the Regiment – the house, that is – for some form of reception to take place at the Manor after a funeral . . .'

'I've heard that they do everything very well over there at Almstone,' murmured Sloan helpfully. It always behoved a policeman to know his own manor – and Manors.

'Carry on, Mr Powell.' The Superintendent was getting restive. He started drumming his fingers on his desk and said, 'Time's getting on.'

'Since we had arrived outside Berebury in such very good time and did not want to go to the Manor first,' Lionel Powell obediently resumed his narrative, 'we – er – decided instead to have a cup of coffee at a roadside café near Cullingoak called Pete's Place.'

'It seemed the only establishment on that road for miles,' sniffed Julia Powell. She was dressed in grey with touches of black, the whole set off by a mauve scarf. The ensemble did nothing for her, decided Sloan. She still looked censorious rather than grieving.

'It is,' said Sloan briefly. Was Lionel Powell going to tell him they'd seen drugs being passed or smelt cannabis being smoked at Pete's Place? Because, if so, it wouldn't be news to Detective Inspector Sloan or, very probably, to almost anyone in the county of Calleshire between the ages of twelve and twenty. And he, Sloan, was certainly not going to explain the carefully laid police plans for Pete and his Place to any passer-by, well intentioned or otherwise, civil servant or not.

'It's not, of course, somewhere we would have chosen,' insisted Lionel Powell, 'had there been any- where else.'

'There isn't,' said Sloan. In fact, had the Powells been actively seeking a culture shock they couldn't have found anywhere better.

'Very insalubrious, we found it,' said Mrs Powell.

'It is, indeed,' agreed Sloan hastily. This was not the pace at which the Superintendent liked state- ments to proceed. 'So?'

'So, we – I, that is, had time in which to open my morning's post . . .'

'And?' prompted Sloan in a gallant attempt to extract the man's story more quickly.

'And found that it included a letter to me from my late mother.'

'Ah . . .' Sloan's gaze swivelled round in the direction of the Superintendent's desk. That explained the letter and its envelope there.

'Posted after her death,' said Lionel Powell impressively.

'In which,' contributed Superintendent Leeyes heavily, 'Mrs Gertrude Powell quite clearly states her belief that someone was attempting to kill her.'

'Someone unnamed?' asked Sloan.

'Some person or persons unnamed,' responded Gertrude Powell's son pedantically. 'She doesn't say who or how many in the letter.'

Suppressing a strong desire to say that the number was immaterial at this stage, it was the fact that mattered, Detective Inspector Sloan moved forward to examine the letter for himself.

'This, I take it, sir, is your mother's handwriting?'

'Undoubtedly,' said Lionel Powell.

The letter was written on Almstone Manor's writing paper in a large flowing hand and began, 'My dear Lionel, By the time you receive this letter I shall be dead . . .'

'There's no date on it,' pointed out Lionel, 'but as you can see the envelope was postmarked in Berebury yesterday.'

Sloan read on. The message was nothing if not melodramatic. ' . . . killed by an unknown hand under a Pragmatic Sanction I didn't want, but free at last to join your poor father.'

'Melodramatic to the end,' said Julia Powell unkindly.

'Do we know, sir, what she meant by Pragmatic Sanction?'

'I don't, for one,' said Lionel Powell. 'Historically it was a political arrangement to ensure the smooth succession of an undivided heritage but I don't think my mother would have known that.'

Sloan, matching the man's own pedantry, asked Lionel if he or his wife themselves had any reason to suppose that someone had accelerated Mrs Gertrude Powell's demise.

'None whatsoever,' Lionel Powell came back quickly. 'The whole idea is perfectly absurd.'

'She's dead, isn't she?' said Julia Powell bleakly. 'Isn't that enough for the police?'

'Had she been dying, though?' countered Sloan. As he understood it, all the residents of the Manor were old and some of them were ill, too.

'She had been unwell for some time,' said Gertie Powell's son, 'and the doctor had told us more than once that she wouldn't live very long.'

'Which doctor?' asked Sloan. There were doctors and doctors in Calleshire, as everywhere else in the world. And, heretical though the belief was thought in some circles to be, some of them were better – much better – at the practice of medicine than others.

Very much better.

'Browne,' said Lionel Powell. 'Dr Angus Browne. We were told he looked after everyone in the Manor and he seemed all right . . . that is, we had no reason to suppose he wasn't.'

Sloan nodded. He knew Dr Angus Browne – a middle-aged Scotsman from over Larking way – and knew, too, that the doctor was no fool.

'He signed my mother's death certificate the day she died,' continued Lionel Powell. 'I went over and collected it myself.'

'And the cause of death given on it?' asked Sloan, noting that the doctor, then, had been happy enough about the old lady's death to certify it as being from natural causes.

'Chronic renal failure.'

Sloan looked sharply at Lionel Powell and then glanced again at the clock. 'Is it a burial or cremation?'

'Burial.'

'I see.' Detective Inspector Sloan took a deep breath and uttered the very words he had never thought he would ever hear himself use to the Superintendent. 'I think, sir, this is a job where I am going to need Detective Constable Crosby . . .'

'Need Crosby?' echoed his superior officer in disbelief. It was a truth universally acknowledged at Berebury Police Station that young Constable Crosby was an incubus in any investigation: more defective than detective. 'Are you quite sure?'

'That's if I'm going to get to Almstone Church in time,' said Detective Inspector Sloan.

The Reverend Adrian Brailsford had mounted the pulpit at St Clement's Church at Almstone with a certain lack of enthusiasm for the job in hand. In the ordinary way he found delivering *oraisons funèbres* no problem, they being as it were part and parcel of his own daily round as the curé of souls in the parish of Almstone in the diocese of Calleford. In fact, sometimes he even quite enjoyed pronouncing them, conscious that not only was he carrying out a last duty towards one of his flock but supporting the mourners, too – and all at the same time as giving full rein to his views on the importance of the Christian message of peace and forgiveness.

But not this morning.

'Dearly beloved brethren,' he enjoined them formally, 'we are gathered here together today to give thanks for the life of Gertrude Eleanor Murton Powell . . .'

Adrian Brailsford had hoped at first that the Regimental Chaplain would have come to Almstone to take this service himself, but that khaki cleric was away on active duty with the Fearnshires somewhere in Europe. All he, Adrian Brailsford, Rector of this parish, had been told about that clergyman's absence was that the Regiment was busy trying to sort out the human cockpit that the Balkans had again become.

'A life,' he went on, picking his words about Gertrude Powell with minefield care, 'which we all know was one lived to the full.' The Rector was well aware that a funeral was usually one of the services at which it was more likely that he had the complete attention of all of his congregation. He could almost feel it from the pulpit now.

'You might say she lived it to the utmost,' he added.

The same interest, alas, could not always be felt from those attending some of the other offices of the church. Sometimes, indeed, at children's services and Harvest Festival time, he wasn't sure that he had their attention at all. Often enough, too, he felt he was a mere figurehead at such occasions as the Christmas Carol Service.

Not today.

Today he had no need to make a conscious effort to stifle any negative thoughts of his own or try to engage the wandering minds of his flock. Today he knew he had the complete attention of everyone present. He laid out his notes on the pulpit rail and turned to address the assembled company on the subject of the life of the deceased.

'It was, of course, only the last few years of that crowded life which she had spent amongst us here in Almstone . . .'

It hadn't been easy for him to find the right

words for his encomium. Adrian's usual wont was to talk first to the relatives about their favourite memory of the deceased and then weave what they had said seamlessly into the fabric of his address, augmenting the tribute as necessary with passing references to the bread of affliction and the waters of sorrow (there being very few people who escaped these two sad experiences in life). However, he had found Lionel Powell notably reticent on the subject of his late mother's past life.

'Varied,' he'd said tersely.

'Ah!'

'Especially in the war.'

'I see. Perhaps, then, you could tell me . . .'

'She did a lot of driving of officers on Salisbury Plain before going out to Egypt with her first husband,' Lionel had volunteered unhelpfully.

With which Adrian Brailsford had had to be content.

Matron, that usually excellent woman, when appealed to in turn, had said judiciously that she had been given to understand that Mrs Gertrude Powell had always lived life to the utmost and had no regrets but more than that she really could not say. Brailsford had seized on the phrase, inviting her to elaborate on it. This, though, Mrs Muriel Peden had signally failed to do.

Instead she had suggested that some of Mrs Powell's old friends at the Manor – Captain Markyate, for instance – might like to talk to him about the old days. The residents, she had added drily, usually preferred talking about the old days to any other days.

This hadn't been as much help to Adrian Brailsford as it might have been because of the unease he always felt when talking to any of the residents of the Manor. It wasn't that they ever made him feel actually unwelcome. Merely not one of them. This dated, he was sure, from a sermon one Sunday in which he had preached on pacifism and the importance of turning the other cheek. On his next visit to the Manor a doughty, bedridden old warrior had invited him to inspect a quite different cheek once penetrated by an enemy bayonet.

When asked by Brailsford about the late Mrs Gertrude Powell, Captain Peter Markyate had hummed and hawed and fussed about with the silver-framed photographs on the mantelshelf of his room while managing to tell the Rector absolutely nothing about the deceased except that she'd been 'a bit of a goer' in her day. 'She used to talk a good deal about a poem she liked called "The Road Not Taken",' he said at last.

'By Robert Frost,' the Rector had helpfully identified it. 'What about it?'

'Gertie used to say she'd taken both roads.' He stirred uncomfortably. 'Well, all roads, actually.' He paused. 'And she had.'

'I see,' said Brailsford, mentally assessing the worth of this as eulogy material.

24

'Of course, she was good-looking, too,' Markyate had added warmly. 'She was very good-looking, then.'

'A widow, I understand,' said Brailsford.

Markyate coughed and murmured something very indistinct about Gertie's first husband, Donald Tulloch, having bought it at Tobruk.

'Ah,' said the Rector, mentally beginning to compose something sonorous but suitable about sacrifice and death in battle. 'And her second husband?'

Peter Markyate stared at his shoes and muttered vaguely that as far as he himself knew no one was absolutely sure exactly what had happened to Gertie's second husband. He didn't think there was anyone who could tell the Rector anything about him now. Anyone at all. Gertie herself never spoke of her second husband.

'Mr Powell, you mean?' said Brailsford.

Captain Markyate shook his head. 'No, no, Rector, Hubert Powell was her third husband,' he said, adding with a sudden burst of energy, 'Thank goodness.'

'Thank goodness?' echoed Brailsford.

'He was the one with the money.'

Chapter Three

There is no armour against Fate

'Where to, sir?' enquired Detective Constable Crosby from the driving seat. He was already revving up the engine of the police car in the yard.

'Almstone,' said Detective Inspector Sloan, adding grudgingly, 'And you can put a shift on if you like.'

'Thank you, sir.' Crosby slammed the engine into gear and the car roared joyously out of the police compound. Driving fast cars fast was his greatest joy in life. 'Trouble, sir?'

'Maybe. Can't say yet,' said Sloan. 'As far as I can see the choice lies between its being all about an old lady with an overdeveloped taste for high drama or real mischief.'

'So where's the fire then?' asked Crosby, heading the car out of the car park at a speed satisfactory to him if to no one else.

'We are going,' said Sloan precisely, 'to St Clement's Church to stop a funeral.'

'That's new, sir,' said the detective constable appreciatively. 'Haven't done that before.' He crouched over the wheel, leaving the streets of Berebury behind with speed. He started to hum the tune of 'Get Me to the Church on Time' under his breath.

'Because Morton's, the undertakers,' remarked Sloan bitterly, 'are probably the only firm in Calleshire not to have a mobile telephone in their business vehicle.'

'Their hearse, you mean?' said Crosby, treating some new traffic-calming installations rather as a champion skier would deal with a tight slalom in a speed race.

'I do.'

'Tod Morton wouldn't risk anything that might wake the dead,' said Crosby, executing a stately pas de deux on the narrow country road with a double-decker bus bound for Calleford. 'Not good for business.'

'And there's no one in at the rectory to step across to the church with a message,' said Sloan, explaining to himself as much as Crosby why they had to rush out in this unseemly way to Almstone. 'By the way, Crosby, in the unlikely event of there being a car following us to the church, it belongs to the son of the deceased.'

'There was one to start with, sir,' admitted Crosby, 'but it's not there any more.'

'I didn't think . . . Look out, man!' Sloan's shutting of his eyes was quite involuntary as a milk float pulled out of a side turning ahead of them.

'There are some drivers who shouldn't be allowed on the road, sir, aren't there?' Crosby was saying equally when he opened them again.

'There are,' gritted Sloan, 'and I am not at all sure, Crosby, that you aren't one of them.' His friend Inspector Harpe of Traffic Division was even more sure on this point. He routinely resisted all of the constable's earnest efforts to transfer from the Criminal Investigation Department to Traffic Division.

'So what's the hurry then, sir?' asked Crosby. 'I mean, Tod's not going to run off with the coffin, is he?'

'The hurry, Crosby, is to get to Almstone church-yard before the deceased is interred.'

'Couldn't we dig the coffin up again if we're too late?' asked Crosby. 'It couldn't harm for a day or so, could it, sir?'

'Not without an exhumation order from the Home Office, we couldn't,' said Sloan.

Detective Constable Crosby, who had been in the Force for quite long enough to equate the Home Office with excessive paperwork, nodded his complete comprehension.

'And when we get back to the station, Crosby,' continued Sloan, 'you can prepare me a report on something called the Pragmatic Sanction. It might improve your driving.' This, he knew, was unfair, but then he had just been badly frightened by a milk float.

'Yes, sir.' He changed gear. 'I know a bit already.'

'You do?' said Sloan, surprised.

'It's what Sergeant Gelven says was taken away from the police by the Crown Prosecution Service. He didn't like that.'

They had rounded the corner into Almstone before Sloan could do more than tuck the fact away in his mind. 'There, Crosby,' he said, leaning forward, 'that's St Clement's Church over there. I can see the tower. Keep going.'

So it fell out that Mrs Maisie Carruthers, still too frail to attend the funeral, but not too immobile to get to the window of her room at the Manor, became the onlooker who saw most of the game. From her first-floor vantage point she was in the best position of all to see the cortège leave the church and start out very slowly towards the newly dug grave space in the south-west corner of the churchyard.

It was led by the Reverend Adrian Brailsford in full canonicals, followed by Tod Morton, young sprig of the firm of Morton and Sons, Funeral Furnishers, complete with silk top hat, black jacket and striped trousers. After them came the first of the mourners, Brigadier Hamish MacIver and Captain Peter Markyate to the fore.

Maisie Carruthers watched, fascinated, as this procession was met on the church path at full trot by two men. Though they were in plain clothes they had nevertheless stepped smartly out of the police car she could see parked by the lich-gate.

What might at first have seemed a classic case of irresistible force meeting immovable object dissolved before Maisie Carruthers' spellbound gaze into what, at that distance, looked for all the world like a discussion group. In the further distance she caught sight of another car with a man at the wheel and a woman beside him approaching the church gate at speed.

After only a moment or two of colloquy Tod Morton, who had recognized Detective Inspector Sloan and Detective Constable Crosby, turned on his heel, took off his top hat and, without more ado, ordered the bearer-party back into the church.

The Rector, on the other hand, who had never seen either policeman before, took refuge in canon law.

'I quite understand, gentlemen,' he said, yielding to the two policemen with quiet dignity. 'Fortunately the Order of Service for the Burial of the Dead provides for a natural interval between the church and the grave.'

'A natural interval, eh, Sloan?' Superintendent Leeyes gave the short bark that did duty with him for a laugh. 'I like the sound of that.'

'Yes, sir.' Duty bound, Detective Inspector Sloan's first action had been to radio back to his superior officer at Berebury Police Station. 'I'm arranging for the church to be locked while the coffin is there.'

'And I, Sloan, have had a word with old Locombe-Stableford . . .'

Mr Locombe-Stableford was Her Majesty's Coroner for East Calleshire and a long-time sparring partner of Superintendent Leeyes.

' . . . and he's cancelled the burial order for the deceased.'

'I'll let the Rector and Tod Morton know that they definitely can't go ahead with the interment now, sir,' said Sloan, 'whatever anyone else may think.'

'And the Coroner's ordered a post-mortem,' added Leeyes. 'So it's up to the pathologist now. We'll see what Dr Dabbe has to say.'

'Yes, sir.'

'Not that that let's us off the hook, of course, Sloan. I hope you realize that.'

'Yes, sir. Naturally.'

'So see what you can do out there at Almstone. Strike while the iron is hot.' He gave another seal-like bark, laughing at his own witticism. 'I say you should catch 'em while they're still at a wake . . . and not asleep.'

'Very good, sir.'

'And keep Crosby with you.'

'Thank you, sir,' Sloan managed to say between

clenched teeth. Detective Constable Crosby was the weakest link in any detection chain.

'Then we shan't have him in our hair over here at the station.'

Chapter Four

Death lays his icy hand on kings

'Lisa, Lisa!' Mrs Muriel Peden shot through the green-baize door of the Manor in search of her cook. 'Where are you?'

As Albert Einstein put it so much better, everything is relative, and as many another victim of crisis has found, relative values can change rapidly. And unexpectedly. Matron was quite surprised to find that her own first steps were taken – like the way of all flesh – in the direction of the kitchen. Her thoughts had flown straight there as she had hurried out of the church and back to the Manor.

While she had sped across the churchyard ahead of the rest of the congregation she had made a swift inventory in her mind of the menu of the excellent cold collation that ought to be – would surely be – awaiting the arrival of the mourners in the old oak-panelled dining room.

'I'm here, Matron.' Lisa Haines, plump and white-aproned, appeared out of the larder, a great dish of smoked salmon in her hands. 'Are they all back? Everything's ready.'

'I'm sure,' murmured Muriel Peden pleasantly, that being the least of her worries. She regarded the fish in a calculating way. Of all of the emotions chasing through her mind at that moment, she was honest enough to admit that it was economy that surfaced.

'And though I says it as shouldn't, Matron,' beamed the cook, 'the table and the sideboard look really lovely. It was meant for proper food, that dining room.'

'And it would be a great pity to waste all of it,' said Mrs Peden, making up her mind on the matter. 'Not right, I mean . . .'

'Waste it?' echoed Lisa, shocked. 'You couldn't do that, Matron. Not all that cooked ham . . . it's home-cured!'

'Which wouldn't freeze.'

'And then there's the cold duck,' said Lisa. 'I did that myself special because Mrs Powell – God rest her poor soul – always liked my duck when it was served. She said so every time.'

'And that wouldn't freeze either,' said Muriel Peden decisively, 'would it?'

'Freeze?' Lisa's starched apron rustled at the very word. 'Why should it be put in the freezer, I'd like to know? They'll be here any minute and if I know them they'll be hungry.'

Resisting the terrible temptation to say that

freezing was probably what was going to happen to the late Mrs Powell – God rest her soul, indeed – Matron explained that there had been police at the funeral.

'Oh, that's no problem, Matron,' responded Lisa immediately. 'I'll give them something in the kitchen.' She looked down at the charger of smoked salmon and its decoration of halves of lemon and subconsciously tightened her grip on it. 'There's plenty of that ham left and there's some beer in the cooler. That'll do for the police.'

'That's not quite what I meant, Lisa,' began Muriel Peden weakly.

'And if I know them, the residents will be quite peckish by now. Some of them have been up for hours getting ready, the darlings.'

Mrs Peden, who held a less rosy view of her charges than did the middle-aged cook, nodded.

'And,' went on Lisa, 'Hazel says she had her hands ever so full with Captain Markyate this morning. He was in such a fret, poor old gentleman, about which tie to put on for the funeral. Ever so upset today, she said he was.'

'He chose the black,' murmured Muriel Peden.

'Ah, but Hazel said she had quite a time with him because he couldn't make up his mind.'

'He never can. . .' said Matron.

'He thought perhaps he should wear the regimental one on account of Mrs Powell's first husband having been in the Fearnshires.'

Matron, an essentially kind woman, made a mental note to remark later to Captain Markyate on the suitability of black.

'Oh, and Mrs Carruthers has just rung to say she's coming down for the luncheon after all.' Lisa pursed her lips. 'I don't know what's made her change her mind, I'm sure.'

'I can guess. . .' began Muriel Peden warmly.

'Said to Hazel when she first came that she was going to stay up in her room until she got used to the place, she did, and that it would be a case of all her meals up there.'

'They all do to begin with,' said Matron absently, her attention distracted by the sight of the first of her flock coming up the drive. She turned back to the door out of the kitchen. 'You'd better serve that smoked salmon right away, Lisa. The Brigadier was going to see to opening the champagne and I expect he's gone right ahead in spite of everything . . . it would be just like him.'

The dilemma experienced by Lionel and Julia Powell was purely a social and not an economic one. It centred on whether in the circumstances they should accept the hospitality of the Manor. This Gordian knot was cut for them by the unlikely combination of the police and their own two daughters.

The former, in the person of Detective Inspector Sloan, had indicated a desire to have further converse in due course with the Powells, and their daughters had flatly refused to miss out on anything in the nature of a champagne luncheon.

'Nonsense, Daddy,' said Amanda to their parents' suggestion that they had something to eat on their way back to London.

'We're starving,' announced Clarissa. 'Do you realize how early we had to get up this morning to get here from town?'

'Besides, Daddy,' said Amanda firmly, 'this is our last chance to find out what Granny was really like.'

'I bet she was fast,' said her sister.

'Clarissa!' exclaimed Julia Powell. 'You shouldn't be talking like that about your grandmother.'

'Why didn't you like us coming down here to see her then?' Amanda challenged her mother. 'You always tried to put us off.'

'There was something that you were keeping from us,' insisted Clarissa dramatically.

'Don't be silly, girls,' snapped Lionel.

'And we mean to find out what it was,' chimed in Amanda. 'Come along, Clary, let's follow the crowd.'

'At least,' said Julia Powell acidly to her husband as they reluctantly trailed behind the other mourners towards the Manor dining room, 'they're not "Following the Band".'

Lionel, who understood the allusion perfectly, pretended not to hear.

*

'A little more ham, Inspector?' The cook's knife hovered over the ample bone set on the old-fashioned variety of china stand not often seen except in a grocer's shop.

'Well . . . I must say it's very good.' The policeman had asked nothing better than a chance to get his feet under the kitchen table at the Manor. 'You don't see a lot of home-cured ham about these days. Now, who was it you said looked after the late Mrs Powell here?'

'Hazel.' Lisa Haines glanced at the door. 'Hazel Finch. She'll be down in a minute. She's feeding Mrs Forbes. Poor lady – she can't even lift a spoon for herself these days.'

'Mrs Powell had been ill for quite a time, too, hadn't she?' murmured Sloan, accepting some proffered chutney.

'Oh, yes.' Lisa Haines nodded vigorously. 'Going downhill for weeks. That's apricot and walnut chutney. I made it myself.'

'It's very good,' said Sloan truthfully. 'Now, about Mrs Powell . . .'

Lisa Haines looked up as the kitchen door opened. 'Ah, here's Hazel. She'll tell you all you want to know about Mrs Powell, Inspector. She looked after her.'

Hazel Finch was a large, slow girl who sank down at the table, one eye on the ham bone and another on the detective inspector.

She agreed ponderously that Mrs Powell had been ill for weeks before she died.

'Were you worried about her?' asked Sloan.

Hazel shook her head. 'No. Matron always promises our ladies and gentlemen that they can die here if they want to and she says we aren't none of us to worry when they do.'

The cook nodded comfortably, placing a substantial plateful of ham in front of the girl. 'And, Inspector, however bad they are, Matron tells them that here there's no hurry about dying.'

'I'm very glad to hear it,' said Sloan astringently. Hurry about dying was something that always worried the Criminal Investigation Department at Berebury.

'If I was like Mrs Forbes upstairs I'd want to die as soon as I could,' volunteered Hazel, tucking in to the ham.

Lisa Haines pushed some mustard in the girl's direction and echoed the sentiment. 'I'm sure I hope someone will put me out of my misery if I ever get as bad as that poor old lady.'

'She can't do anything for herself,' said Hazel, making immediate inroads in the ham. 'Anything at all. It's a shame.'

'Of course she could die at any time,' said the cook. 'She does know that.'

'About Mrs Powell . . .' said Sloan valiantly.

'She didn't need no help until the end,' said Hazel between mouthfuls.

'Ah . . !' said Sloan, whose professional concern was that Mrs Gertie Powell hadn't had the wrong sort of help towards the end. He drew breath and took a long shot: 'So when did she give you the letter, Hazel?'

''Bout a month ago.' The big girl didn't even pause before she answered. 'I remember because it was just before I went on my holiday. Mrs Powell gave me some money for that and then gave me a letter.'

'Another slice of ham, Inspector?' Lisa's knife hovered above the ham bone. 'I'll have to get started on dishing up the desserts any minute now.'

Wordlessly, Sloan passed his plate, his eye still on Hazel Finch.

'Then Mrs Powell,' resumed Hazel Finch, 'asked me if anything happened to her would I post that letter.'

'Did she tell you when you were to post it?' asked Sloan.

'Oh, yes.' Hazel nodded. 'She was most particular about that. She said it was to go into the pillar box outside Almstone post office the day before her funeral.' She finished a large mouthful and then went on, 'You see, she wanted her son to have it on the day to cheer him up at the funeral.'

'Nice, that, wasn't it?' said the warm-hearted Lisa Haines sentimentally.

'So she wasn't expecting to go while you were

away?' said the detective inspector to Hazel, leaving aside the question of whether what Mrs Powell had done – if she had – was nice.

'Oh, no.' Hazel Finch shook her head quite vigorously. 'Promised me she'd still be there shocking everyone when I got back.'

'And she was?'

'Lived another fortnight.' She grinned. 'Ever such a naughty lady, she was really . . . but nice with it, if you know what I mean.'

Detective Inspector Sloan said truthfully that he knew exactly what she meant. And he did, although the naughty people he usually dealt with were anything but nice. Downright nasty, most of them: unprincipled, violent, greedy, selfish, murderous perhaps.

'You're going to miss her, Hazel,' opined Lisa Haines.

'She was fun,' pronounced the care assistant.

As epitaphs went, thought Sloan, it couldn't easily be bettered.

Out in the churchyard Detective Constable Crosby was making the revised arrangements for the disposal of the dead with Tod Morton, the undertaker.

'She's to go over to Berebury Hospital for Dr Dabbe,' the constable said.

'Ah, a post-mortem case,' said young Tod

knowledgeably. 'Thought as much the moment I set eyes on you and the Inspector. Don't often see the police at a funeral.'

'And pretty pronto, please,' added Crosby.

'Trouble?'

'Could be,' said Crosby.

'Cutting it a bit fine, weren't you?' said Tod curiously.

'No,' said Crosby.

'Another ten minutes and we'd have had her six feet under.'

'Ten minutes is ten miles,' said Crosby ineluctably.

'Not in a hearse, it isn't,' rejoined Tod. 'You police've got your regulation two and half miles an hour on the beat and we've got—'

'The doctor,' Crosby interrupted him, 'is waiting.'

The undertaker waved a hand in the direction of the south-west corner of the graveyard. 'So is the lady's lair . . .'

'Her what?'

'Lair.' Tod Morton jerked his shoulder in the direction of the Manor. 'The Fearnshires are a Scottish regiment.'

'So?'

'A lair is what the Scots call a plot in a churchyard,' said the undertaker. 'When they've paid for it, that is.'

'That's as maybe,' said the constable magisterially, 'but as far as the deceased is concerned let me tell you that though it's usually a case of "ashes to ashes" the dust will have to wait for it.'

Chapter Five

Sceptre and Crown
Must tumble down

Mrs Muriel Peden surveyed the dining room of the Manor with a practised eye. She was trying to judge to a nicety the right moment to give the signal for the first course to be cleared away. This was not easy because on the whole her charges were quick drinkers and slow eaters.

For instance, to her certain knowledge Miss Henrietta Bentley, who was still toying with the last of her salad, had already put away two glasses of champagne and one and a half of a good white wine carefully chosen by the Cellar Committee.

Miss Bentley, quite unaware that it was she who was delaying the proceedings, was bending an ear towards little Mrs McBeath.

'I just don't think it's quite nice, that's all,' said Mrs McBeath, greatly daring.

'It's a very fine wine,' said Miss Bentley, draining her glass appreciatively – but not alas attending to her plate. 'An Australian Chardonnay, unless I'm very much mistaken.' The Manor's Cellar Committee

44

had recently ventured out of France and into another hemisphere.

'Not the wine. I meant,' twittered Mrs McBeath, 'our having this luncheon with poor Mrs Powell not yet in her grave.'

'Thrift, thrift, Horatio,' boomed Miss Bentley, daughter of a First World War general and in her day the headmistress of a famous girls' school run on strictly military lines.

Little Mrs McBeath, who didn't recognize the quotation, shied nervously away. Fearful that the formidable Miss Bentley might be expecting a suitable response, she scuttled across the dining room and happened to fetch up alongside Mrs Maisie Carruthers, who was being closely questioned by Clarissa Powell.

'What was Granny really like?' asked that young woman with every appearance of genuine earnestness. 'That's what we want to know.'

Mrs Carruthers considered this carefully, searching for an epithet that was both truthful and suitable for a member of the deceased's family who was of tender years. 'Fun,' she said at last, suppressing all mention of a certain occasion in wartime Cairo. That had been the evening when Gertie had set out to respond to a bet and prove that Egyptians weren't the only girls who could belly dance. 'Your grandmother was always fun.'

Maisie's son, Ned, would scarcely have recognized her as the shrivelled little old lady he'd last seen languishing in the hospital. Clutching an elegant ebony-handled cane, and dressed in her best, Maisie Carruthers' whole appearance now projected a lively interest in the world.

'In what way exactly?' persisted Clarissa, misguidedly imagining that fun then was so very different from fun now. 'Do tell me.'

'Cheerful,' hedged Maisie Carruthers. 'She never let things get her down did Gertie.' She herself was feeling remarkably bobbish just now especially as, wise in her generation, Matron had sent in the hairdresser that very morning.

'What things?'

Here Maisie Carruthers became vague. 'Oh, husbands and that sort of thing.'

'Tell me more,' commanded Clarissa as the diminutive Mrs McBeath decided to leave them both in favour of a less hectic conversation with the Rector.

Across the room Clarissa's sister, Amanda, was chatting up Brigadier MacIver. He was giving her a man's view of the deceased. 'Your dear grandmother was a great character, my dear. And a sad loss to us all at the Manor . . .'

'Do tell me all about her,' pleaded Amanda. 'Please.'

'Just as the Regiment was diminished all those years ago by the death of her husband in action,' said the Brigadier sonorously.

'Which husband?' asked Amanda, every bit as forthright as her sister.

'Her first.'

'Did they have any children? I mean, has Daddy got stepbrothers and sisters that we don't know about?' She pulled her face down in a grimace. 'The parents won't ever talk about granny's past.'

'Quite, quite,' coughed the Brigadier. 'No, she and Donald Tulloch didn't have any children. No time. Not then. There was a war on, you see.'

'And her second husband?'

The Brigadier plunged his face into his wine glass and mumbled, 'Never mentioned.'

'How romantic.'

'Probably not,' said the old soldier.

'Any children that time round?'

'She never said. Not one to talk, Gertie,' said Hamish MacIver. In fact, Gertie had always been famously discreet in some matters as well as at one and the same time being famously indiscreet about others, but he saw no reason to tell her grand-daughter this.

Amanda sighed. 'Then there was Tertius, I suppose.'

'Who?'

'Her third husband. Tertius means third,' she explained kindly. 'Latin and all that. My grandfather.'

'Ah, yes, of course,' he said. 'Hubert Powell.'

'And they had poor old dull Daddy . . .'

The Brigadier assented to this with a little bow but without comment.

'How unromantic,' said Amanda.

Privately the Brigadier agreed with her. There was precious little of Gertie in her son Lionel. 'We don't choose our parents, m'dear. Just have to make the best of those we get.'

'It's not easy,' said Amanda frankly, looking towards the window, where her own father and mother were standing as much apart from the residents as they decently could. The Reverend Adrian Brailsford, noting their isolation and at the same time seeing an opportunity of shaking off Mrs Morag McBeath, had set off in their direction.

'No,' agreed the Brigadier.

'And what happens now?' asked Amanda with all the impatience of youth.

The Brigadier said he was blessed if he really knew. 'I expect,' he murmured without thinking, 'they'll just keep everything on ice for a bit.'

'I bet Daddy loses his cool, though,' forecast Amanda, not sounding at all daunted at the prospect.

'Taking their time, aren't they?' complained Hazel Finch in the kitchen. She'd finished her ham and was sitting back in her chair, looking round expectantly.

'You wait until you're the Judge's age, my girl,' said Lisa Haines warmly, 'and you won't be bolting your food either.' She turned to Detective Inspector Sloan. 'Ninety, he is and all his own teeth still.'

Detective Inspector Sloan, who had long since ceased to marvel at anything – anything at all – in the human condition save man's inhumanity to man, duly expressed wonderment.

'He's always slow,' said the cook, 'and that Miss Bentley will talk and not eat.'

'How come a judge gets to come here?' asked Sloan. 'Was he in the Fearnshires, too?' Privately he resolved to have a quiet word with Judge whoever he was and find out if he had kept all his marbles as well as his teeth.

'He was an army judge,' said the cook, disappearing into the larder and emerging with two large bowls of chocolate mousse. She set them down on the sideboard and went back for two decorated trifles. 'There, I'm ready when they are.'

Hazel Finch followed the progress of the desserts across the room with her eyes like a hungry child. 'Look lovely, don't they?'

'The first bite is with the eye,' said the cook knowledgeably. 'There's a *tarte aux pommes* as well but if I know anything they won't touch it.'

Detective Inspector Sloan, always ready to enlarge his store of esoteric information, crime having no boundaries – no boundaries at all – enquired with genuine interest, 'Why a tart at all if they won't eat it?'

'So they know there's more. That way they'll finish the mousse and the trifle without worrying.' She jerked a shoulder in the direction of the dining room. 'Brought up to leave something for Mr Manners, most of 'em.'

Sloan, who had been brought up by an economical mother to eat everything that was put in front of him and by a police training to take every opportunity of assessing a situation from all angles, offered to give the cook a hand with taking the puddings through to the dining room when the time came.

Hazel Finch was worrying about something quite different. 'I don't like that French apple tart.'

'I've kept a trifle back,' remarked the cook to no one in particular, adding enigmatically, 'Better safe than sorry.'

'Makes a lot of extra, doesn't it?' said Sloan, anxious to get the conversation back to the late Mrs Powell. 'An occasion like this coming out of the blue . . .'

Lisa Haines shook her head. 'We're used to it. There was the funeral luncheon for Mrs Chalmers-Hyde last month.'

'I don't miss her,' said Hazel. 'Not like I shall miss Mrs Powell.'

'And then we had a big party the other week, Inspector,' said the cook. 'For the Judge's ninetieth.'

'Ever so excited everyone was, about that,' contributed Hazel, the supply of her next course now safely assured.

'And his birthday surprise really knocked him sideways, I can tell you,' chimed in the cook. 'I saw his face and he was shaken rigid.'

At which moment the bell marked 'dining room' jangled on the board.

Muriel Peden was still keeping her eye on the serving of food. She noted with relief that, at long last, without anyone on hand to talk to, Miss Bentley had swallowed the remainder of her salad. The old lady then sat back and surveyed the splendid oak-panelled dining room with a beady eye. Looking round she saw only Matron within earshot, which was perhaps just as well.

'What's she doing here?' Miss Bentley demanded, pointing her stick in the direction of Walter Bryant, round whose wheelchair a visitor – Miss Margot Ritchie – was now fluttering like an anxious butterfly. 'Mark my words, Matron, before you can say "knife" it'll be another case of "the funeral baked meats coldly furnishing the marriage feast".' She sniffed loudly. 'And we all know what became of Hamlet's mother, don't we?'

Since Muriel Peden had no satisfactory response to this she simply opened her hands in a gesture of agreement with the validity of the quotation.

'No better than she ought to be,' declared Miss Bentley uncompromisingly.

'Mr Bryant may invite anyone whom he wishes to the Manor,' murmured the Matron.

'It isn't his funeral,' said Miss Bentley ineluctably.

'Miss Ritchie was at the service, too,' she pointed out weakly.

Miss Bentley exploded. 'She didn't even know Mrs Powell like we did.'

'As a friend of Mr Bryant's . . .'

'That's one way of describing her,' said the old headmistress darkly. 'Wait until his daughters get to know she's been here again.'

Muriel Peden sighed. She knew exactly what it was that Walter Bryant's two daughters were afraid of . . . their father's getting married again.

'If you ask me,' said Miss Bentley, 'that woman's well and truly got her claws into him.'

'She did send some flowers to the Manor for after the funeral.' The Matron pointed to a display of red and white roses, quite eye-catching against the dark linenfold panelling of the ancient dining room.

'You shouldn't have let them put them in here,' said Miss Bentley, scarcely turning her head. 'Most unsuitable.'

'Why not?' protested Muriel Peden.

'Red and white,' she said sternly.

'But . . .'

'Blood and bandages.' Miss Bentley sniffed. 'Those flowers are in even worse taste than one of Morag McBeath's stitchings.'

'Embroidery,' Muriel Peden corrected her. 'And very nice it is, too. Mrs McBeath is very skilled with her needle.'

Miss Bentley uttered something perilously close

to a snort and then waved her stick in another direction. 'Are those two young girls Gertie's grand-daughters? Because if so, you'd better divert the Judge's attention. He hasn't taken his eyes off them yet and he looks to me as if he's getting thoroughly overexcited.' She brought her walking stick back to the carpet with a bang. 'Which is more than can be said for Captain Markyate. Ever.'

'You'll have to excuse me, Miss Bentley.' Matron took a deep breath and reminded herself for the hundredth time of the generation gap between herself and her charges. 'I must ring for the next course. Everyone's ready now.'

'Goody, goody,' said Amanda Powell when it came. 'I simply adore chocolate mousse.' She looked solemnly up at the Brigadier. 'They say chocolate gives you spots but it doesn't.'

'Of course not,' said that old soldier gallantly.

'They only say that,' said Amanda matter-of-factly, 'because actually chocolate helps love along.'

'Really?' he said. There was clearly more of Gertie in the girl than he'd given her credit for.

'And so naturally they don't want you to have any.' There was no doubt about who 'they' were in this context. Involuntarily Amanda's glance had swung in the direction of the window embrasure where, still slightly apart from the throng of residents, Lionel and Julia Powell were engaged in stilted conversation with the Rector.

'Shame,' twinkled the Brigadier to Amanda, beginning to enjoy himself at long last.

'Do you know,' she asked ingenuously, 'what the name Amanda stands for?'

He bent forward. 'Tell me.'

'Love.'

'You don't say . . .'

'They said Granny was very pleased when she was told that was what I was to be called.'

'She knew all about love,' said Hamish MacIver gruffly. 'Almost too much, you might say.'

'I didn't think anyone could know too much about love,' said a wide-eyed Amanda.

'Didn't you, m'dear? Well, take it from an old soldier that you can.'

'Oh, do tell me!' Amanda advanced a little nearer to the Brigadier and lowered her voice into an mellifluous gurgle. 'You sound like One Who Knows . . .'

It had been no part of Detective Inspector Sloan's plans to intrude upon the Manor's dining-room party at this stage but an old-fashioned courtesy as well as downright police curiosity demanded that he open the door for Lisa Haines, burdened as she was with a tray of bowls of dessert reinforcements. First he saw nothing but a sociable gathering but then he noticed an abrupt change in the room's atmosphere.

He sensed rather than saw a sudden stillness descend upon the room's occupants. At the same time a silence fell, broken only by a woman fussing round the rugs of a man in a wheelchair. Sloan was aware, though, that the only other movement came from those who fell back slightly to clear the way for a woman clutching an elegant ebony-handled cane as she advanced upon a distinguished-looking elderly man apparently deep in conversation with a pretty young girl. It was, he felt, as if everyone else there was holding their collective breath while a confrontation took place.

'Well, Hamish . . .' said Mrs Maisie Carruthers.

'Well, Maisie,' said Brigadier Hamish MacIver.

'It's been a long time.'

'A long, long time.'

'Sir, sir.' Someone was tugging urgently at Sloan's sleeve. 'Sir, please can you come?'

He turned, missing the rest of the scene in the dining room, to see his detective constable standing directly under the head of a stag fixed to the wall above his head. 'Well, what is it, Crosby?'

'The pathologist says he's waiting to start the post-mortem on Gertrude Powell now, sir.'

The detective constable had kept his voice down but the Matron had heard him. She, too, slid quietly out of the dining room and into the corridor, closing the door behind her.

'I'm sorry, madam,' explained Sloan, 'but we've got to go now.' He hesitated. 'We will have to come back, you understand.'

'I think you should,' said Muriel Peden unexpectedly.

Sloan looked up.

'I didn't say anything before,' the Matron murmured awkwardly, 'because I couldn't imagine that it could be important.'

'Circumstances alter cases,' said Crosby prosaically.

'But now . . .' she said as if the constable hadn't spoken.

'Now?' said Sloan.

'Now, I think you ought to know, Inspector,' she said, 'that I – we, that is – have reason to believe that someone may have been into Mrs Powell's room very soon after she'd died.'

'Been into?'

'All right then,' she conceded unwillingly, the word almost wrung out of her, 'searched.'

Chapter Six

And in the dust be equal made
With the poor crookèd scythe and spade

'And what have we here, Sloan, may I ask?' said Dr H.S. Dabbe, Consultant Pathologist to the Berebury and District Hospitals Trust, by way of welcome to the two policemen standing in the mortuary. His taciturn assistant, Burns, was already helping him into his green operating gown.

'Body of a female aged eighty-two,' responded Detective Inspector Sloan, 'who died six days ago.'

'And what brings you two here as well?' Dr Dabbe raised his eyebrows quizzically as he started to tug on his rubber boots.

'A written allegation by the deceased,' said Sloan succinctly, 'that she had been murdered.'

'Well, well.' The pathologist grinned and said, 'We don't get a lot of self-referrals in this branch of medical practice. Come to that, Sloan, I don't get many people brought in here in a shroud. You two been body snatching?'

'Only in a manner of speaking,' said Sloan,

explaining the circumstances. 'Her name is Gertrude Eleanor Murton Powell.'

Dr Dabbe reached for a form. 'Place of death?'

'The Manor at Almstone.'

The doctor's pen hovered above the paper. 'Where did you say?'

'The Manor at Almstone,' repeated Sloan, adding, 'I believe that technically speaking its classification is as a residential care and nursing home for the elderly.'

'One of God's waiting rooms,' said Crosby. In the constable's book, decrepitude set in soon after the age of thirty.

'The Manor at Almstone . . .' Dr Dabbe frowned. 'That rings a bell, you know.'

Under his breath Crosby chanted, 'Oranges and lemons, said the bells of St Clement's.'

Sloan decided he hadn't heard this and raised an enquiring eyebrow towards the pathologist. At this moment anything – anything at all – to do with the Manor and its residents might be of interest. 'It does, doctor?' he said encouragingly.

'It's coming back to me now. What it was,' the pathologist said, 'if I remember rightly, was that I did rather an odd post-mortem on someone from there not very long ago.'

'You did?' Sloan leaned forward, all attention now. Dr Dabbe always remembered rightly.

'Burns,' called out the pathologist, 'get me the bought ledger, will you, there's a good chap.'

'The office of the dead,' intoned Crosby. 'That's where we are.'

Dr Dabbe ignored this. 'I can't remember the woman's name, not off the top of my head.'

'Odd, did you say?' Detective Inspector Sloan, policeman first, last and very nearly all the time, seized on the important word in their exchange without difficulty.

'All right, then, Sloan,' said the pathologist easily. 'Have it your own way. Shall we say instead that it was slightly unusual?'

'In what way exactly, doctor?'

'Actually, Sloan, now I come to think about it, it was odd in two ways,' said Dr Dabbe as his assistant advanced, bearing a heavy old leather-bound volume. 'Thank you, Burns. Let me see now . . .' The pathologist ran a bony finger down a list. 'Don't get any wrong ideas about this book, Sloan. They may make us keep records on computer here but they can't stop us keeping our own as well. Yet. So we still keep this book going, just to be on the safe side . . . Ah, here we are.' He looked up. 'I thought so . . . on the twelfth of last month I performed an autopsy on one Maude Chalmers-Hyde, a female aged seventy-nine, of the Manor at Almstone.'

'You said unusual in two ways,' Sloan prompted him. They had computers down at the police station, too – and practically everywhere else as well – but he agreed with the pathologist. There was no substitute for the good old-fashioned handwritten policeman's notebook. Concentrated the mind, did a pencil.

'Unusual in one way, Sloan,' said the pathologist, 'because it was requested by the deceased's general practitioner.'

'Ah,' rejoined Detective Inspector Sloan. 'So that's out of the ordinary, I take it?'

'It is when the patient's reached that age, multiple pathology being very common by then. Mind you,' added Dabbe, 'the doctor in this case was Angus Browne of Larking and he's a stickler for having everything right.'

Sloan, upholder of law and order as well as accuracy, said he was glad to hear it.

'He refused to sign the death certificate,' said Dr Dabbe, 'and that meant the Coroner ordered a postmortem.'

'Did he now?' Sloan pulled out his pencil and notebook. 'Tell me more.'

'The family were very cut up about it,' murmured Dr Dabbe, 'and said so.'

'I'm sure they were,' said Sloan smoothly. Pretty nearly all the families they dealt with in F Division of the Calleshire County Constabulary were cut up about something either literally or metaphorically. He didn't know which was the worse for a policeman to have to deal with.

'So you cut up the patient instead?' contributed Detective Constable Crosby, who didn't like attending post-mortems and was not averse to any delay in their starting.

'I did,' responded Dr Dabbe before Sloan could speak to the constable about what someone had once called 'proper words in proper places'.

'And?' said the detective inspector.

'And this is where it was quite unusual in another way,' said Dr Dabbe cheerfully.

'Tell me,' said Sloan.

'Because,' said the pathologist solemnly, 'my post-mortem findings agreed completely with the cause of death diagnosed by her general practitioner but which he had declined to certify to that effect.'

'Not common?'

'I shouldn't like to have to tell you how uncommon,' said Dr Dabbe. 'Not suitable for your young ears. Besides, it might shake your faith in the medical profession or something.'

'So why had the doctor wanted a post-mortem for this Maude Chalmers-Hyde then?' persisted Crosby with the innocent air of one just wanting to get everything straight.

'Because,' said the pathologist neatly, 'Angus Browne hadn't thought she was quite ready to die from the condition from which she had been suffering at the precise moment when she did.'

Sloan hunted for the right word.

'Untimely?'

'He thought, like Macbeth, that "she should have died hereafter",' said Dabbe.

'When you got to go, you got to go,' said Crosby to nobody in particular.

'General practitioners get quite good at judging that sort of thing after a time, you know,' remarked Dr Dabbe. 'Most of 'em develop a feel for knowing when death is nigh.'

'Practice makes perfect,' said Crosby sententiously.

'Now then, Sloan,' said Dr Dabbe, pulling on a green cap, 'are you going to tell me what Angus Browne was quite happy to say this patient died from or am I supposed to make an educated guess?'

Detective Inspector Sloan unfolded a copy of the death certificate that Lionel Powell had given him. 'Chronic renal failure secondary to hypertension.'

'Well, that shouldn't be too difficult to demonstrate one way or the other for starters,' said Dabbe. 'Right, Burns, I'm ready now.'

'I'll be with you as soon as I can,' Mrs Muriel Peden promised the Powells, withdrawing rapidly. 'If you'll excuse me, I have some things I must attend to first.'

She had established Lionel and Julia Powell on their own in a small sitting room well away from the more stalwart of the residents still occupying the dining room. Julia Powell sank thankfully into an easy chair.

'Trust your mother,' said Julia bitterly as soon as the door had closed behind the Matron, 'to be embarrassing right to the end.' She was really wondering if it would be in order for her to slip her shoes off in here. She compromised by carefully easing her right foot out of its tight black patent-leather casing.

'She could always be trusted to do that,' said Lionel with a notable absence of filial piety.

'She couldn't even die quietly.' Julia let out a deep sigh as the shoe came off. 'Ah . . . that's better.'

'She was in a coma for three days,' pointed out Lionel with meticulous accuracy.

'I didn't mean that.' The relief of taking her right shoe off was so great that Julia promptly kicked off the left one too. 'I meant she couldn't die – well – decently like everyone else.'

'But . . .'

'You know what I mean, Lionel, and it's no use your pretending you don't.'

He answered the thought rather than her words. 'We can't get away from the letter whatever we do.'

'It might just have been your mother's idea of a joke,' said Julia Powell, her face flushed with champagne.

'It might,' he agreed cautiously.

'You know what she was like.'

'Only too well,' he groaned. 'Incorrigible. Absolutely incorrigible.'

'I wouldn't put it past her myself,' said Julia Powell, aided by generous quantities of white wine as well as champagne.

'Neither would I,' admitted Lionel morosely.

'And,' Julia Powell almost wailed, 'we still can't find it.'

'No.'

'Are you quite sure they've given you all her papers?'

'How can I be sure?' he asked. 'How can anyone be sure? Her letters have all gone . . . and as to who took them and why, it's anyone's guess.'

'After all,' she said as if he had not spoken, 'you are one of your mother's executors.'

'That, at least,' he said with a touch of irony, 'is not in any doubt.'

She sank back in the chair. 'Well, Lionel, what are you going to do about it?'

'I'm not sure.'

Julia sighed in pure exasperation. Lionel's responses were always literal.

He said gloomily, 'We must accept the fact that we may never find it.'

'Your mother was married to someone after her first husband was killed . . .'

'So she always said.'

' . . . and before she met your father.'

'Before she *married* my father,' Lionel corrected her automatically. 'She may have met him before.'

Julia dismissed this as hair-splitting and got straight to the point. 'Well, why can't we find out who?'

Lionel Powell steepled his fingers very much as

he did in the office when he was composing his thoughts before commencing dictating an important memorandum. 'Because, my dear, we do not know the country in which this . . . alliance . . . took place.'

'If it did,' she bounced back at him.

'Exactly.' He started to enumerate points on his fingers. 'First of all we have no real evidence that she did marry someone else.'

'She always said she had.'

'That, Julia, as I have said many times before, is not evidence.'

'But . . .'

'What my mother said was always – let us say – imaginative but unreliable.'

'You don't have to tell me that,' snapped his wife. 'And what about the famous Tulloch treasure that she was always talking about? How do we know that it – whatever it might have been – ever existed?'

'We don't.'

'Have you ever seen anything that might have been it?'

'Never,' said Lionel.

'Neither have I.' She sniffed. 'And if it's jewellery that she hadn't wanted me to have, which I can quite understand . . .' It was something she couldn't actually understand at all and paused for her husband to protest at this, but he didn't so she hurried on, ' . . . you'd have thought she'd at least have shown it to the girls. She was fond enough of them.'

'You would.'

'So, if it still exists, where is it?'

'She might,' said Lionel, 'have left it in the bank or in a safe deposit somewhere. But there isn't a receipt with her things.'

'That doesn't prove anything, does it?'

He replied mildly, 'It makes it more difficult to locate though.'

'She was always boasting about the things different men had given her,' said Julia with distaste.

'I don't think she married them all,' he said drily. 'And for what it's worth, my father told me that she was absolutely penniless – really down on her beam ends – when he married her, so everything would have been gone by then in any case.'

'It's all your father's fault anyway,' said Julia obscurely.

Lionel made no attempt to deny this or to try to explain all over again that his father had left his entire personal estate to his widow for sound fiscal reasons.

'Well then, who did she marry and why is it so important now?'

'As to who it was, we don't know. All she would ever say is that he was called Tommy Atkins.'

'A euphemism for a soldier . . .'

'Exactly. Although,' he added, 'for what it's worth, when she married my father she was calling herself Smith, because that's what's on their marriage certificate and we've got a copy of that.'

'So,' persisted Julia for the umpteenth time, 'why is it so important?'

'Because in her will everything is to be divided equally between all her heirs of the body female whether legitimate or not and then their heirs.'

'That's you.'

'And any other children she may have had.'

Julia sat up very straight. 'You mean we – you – won't get everything?'

'Not if she had other children.'

'Children?'

'The more the less merry,' said Lionel neatly. The memoranda which emanated from his desk at work were renowned throughout the department for their pithiness.

'But we don't know . . .'

'No.'

'So, Lionel,' her voice had sunk to almost a whisper now, 'as things stand we may never know.'

'That, my dear, is precisely what I am afraid of.'

'But that means . . .'

'It means,' he interrupted her harshly, 'that it'll take years and years to prove one way or the other and that in the meantime we'll be at the mercy of every Tom, Dick and Harry of a claimant.'

She gave a bibulous half-laugh. 'Tommy, anyway.'

Chapter Seven

Some men with swords may reap the field

'What I want to know, Sloan,' said Superintendent Leeyes grumpily, 'is who precisely is having who on?'

'That, sir,' murmured Detective Inspector Sloan, 'is something I can't begin to say.' He was telephoning back to Berebury Police Station from the pathologist's office at the hospital mortuary, a draft copy of the post-mortem examination report in his hand.

'Don't trust me, I'm a doctor,' misquoted Leeyes with relish.

'Not,' Sloan qualified his own last remark, 'at this stage, anyway.'

'And I suppose,' said Leeyes, 'that our friendly neighbourhood pathologist is hedging his bets as usual?'

Sloan addressed himself to the telephone; he found for some reason that he was doing this standing to attention. 'All I can say, sir, is that Dr Dabbe has reported that the cause of death as certified by the deceased's general practitioner would appear to be correct.'

'That,' remarked Leeyes trenchantly, 'wasn't what the deceased said in her letter. She said she was going to be murdered.'

Sloan forged on. 'The pathologist confirms that the late Gertrude Powell had at the time of her demise been suffering from chronic renal failure and hypertension as stated.'

'Suffering from,' said Leeyes gnomically, 'is not the same thing as dying from.'

'Indeed not,' agreed Sloan, continuing his reading aloud. 'In addition to the foregoing he states that the deceased also had had some osteoarthritis and arteriosclerosis which, however, were not contributory factors to her death.'

'Bandying words, as usual,' pronounced the Superintendent, 'that's what he's doing.'

'Furthermore, Dr Dabbe says he has removed organs and tissue for analysis.'

'Buying time,' said Leeyes uncharitably.

'But until the histology is known,' quoted Sloan, 'the report cannot be completed.'

'Will not be completed,' said the Superintendent, 'is what he means.'

Sloan said nothing. For one brief inglorious academic term the Superintendent had attended an evening Adult Education course entitled 'English as She is Spoke'. His premature departure from the class had come, after a preliminary skirmish over the gerund, as a direct result of a total inability to see eye to eye with the course tutor on the proper use of (to say nothing of the difference between) the words 'will' and 'shall'.

The sentence which the unlucky teacher had chosen to illustrate the correct usage was 'I shall drown and no one will save me.' He had unfortunately contrasted this with the less grammatically correct 'I will drown and no one shall save me.'

It was at this point that the dominie had parted company for ever with Superintendent Leeyes. That worthy had insisted that since this latter sentiment perfectly expressed the real intention of all the suicides in the River Calle whom he had ever known, the meaning was quite clear and thus could not possibly be bad English whatever the teacher said . . .

'So where do we go from here, Sloan?' his superior officer was asking now.

'Back to the Manor at Almstone, sir, for a word with the Matron there,' said Sloan. 'After, that is, I've seen Dr Angus Browne over at Larking.'

'There's a sight too many medics about for my liking,' Leeyes sniffed. 'They always agree with each other too much and if they don't, they don't ever say.'

'There is just one other thing, sir . . .'

'Yes?'

'I'd like some background on one of the other residents there. A Judge Calum Gillespie.'

'Never heard of him.'

'Nor me, sir.'

Leeyes brightened. 'An impostor?'

'Seeing as he's now ninety I expect it's only a case of his having been before our time, sir.'

'I collect senile judges, Sloan, and blind and deaf ones.'

'I suspect that this one's just plain old,' said Sloan, touched by a certain melancholy.

Judge Calum Gillespie was indeed old, and the blue veins on the backs of his hands stood out rather like the blue veins do in ripe cheese and certainly those hands were very unsteady, but he was not blind, deaf or senile. Nor had he forgotten the interrogation skills he had learned long ago.

First, looking rather like an elderly tortoise, he thrust his neck out of his collar and let his gaze travel slowly round his sitting room, resting in turn on each of the three other men there. Then he regarded the little gathering for a long moment before speaking.

'And why, pray,' he asked at last, 'was Mrs Powell's funeral stopped?'

Hamish MacIver shook his head. 'Blessed if I know, Calum.'

Walter Bryant inched his electric wheelchair backwards. 'Nor me.' He frowned. 'Funny business, altogether.'

'Don't understand it at all,' murmured the Brigadier.

Captain Peter Markyate sounded peevish. 'Gertie always was totally unpredictable. Always.'

'I don't see what that's got to do with it,' objected Walter Bryant. 'It's not her fault that she died.'

'I take it, gentlemen, that it's not anyone's fault that she died.' The Judge continued his scrutiny of the faces of the other three men. 'Is it?'

'No, no,' they chorused.

'Am I to understand then,' said the Judge, 'that the doctor issued the death certificate in the ordinary way?'

'Oh, yes,' nodded the Brigadier, easing his gammy leg from one position to another. 'At least, we didn't hear that he didn't.'

'Not like with Maude Chalmers-Hyde,' said Captain Markyate.

Walter Bryant nodded. 'You know, don't you, Calum, that Dr Browne didn't write one when she died?'

'Wouldn't do it,' chimed in MacIver. 'Not even when the family pressed him.'

'They couldn't have found anything wrong with Maude's death, though, at the post-mortem,' said Walter Bryant, looking round at the others, 'could they? I mean anything wrong, apart from what she had been suffering from.'

The Judge turned his basilisk stare on the man

in the wheelchair. 'Was there anything else wrong to find?'

'No, no,' said Walter Bryant hastily. 'I'm sure there wasn't.'

'Dr Browne wasn't sure,' said Judge Gillespie ineluctably, 'so why should you have been?'

Bryant looked flustered and covered his confusion by fiddling with the controls on his wheelchair. 'Because she'd been ill for ages and ages.'

'Elizabeth Forbes has been more ill for much longer and hasn't died,' pointed out the Judge.

'Gertie was different,' blurted out Markyate. 'Always.'

The Judge turned in his direction. 'In what way precisely?'

Markyate was saved from replying to this by the entrance of Hazel Finch pushing a tea trolley. She said, 'I'm surprised that any of you can eat anything at all after that lovely lunch.'

'Taste is one of the last faculties to go, m'dear,' said the Judge, leaning forward to lift the lid off a chafing dish. 'Ah, hot anchovy toast.' He let the lid fall back out of his tremulous grasp with a clatter. 'Good.'

Walter Bryant said piously, 'Miss Ritchie doesn't think I should have too much butter. Bad for the heart.'

'Bah!' exploded the Brigadier vigorously. 'The only thing wrong with your heart, Bryant, is that it's in the wrong place. You should know better at your age.'

'Now, then, no fighting,' said Hazel. 'Let's see . . . who's going to be mother and pour the tea?' She ran a swift assessing eye over the group. 'I think it had better be you, Captain Markyate, if you don't mind.'

'The late Gertrude Powell, officer?' Dr Angus Browne's bushy eyebrows lifted enquiringly. 'What about her?'

'Did you,' asked Detective Inspector Sloan, 'have any reservations about certifying the cause of her death?'

'None.'

Sloan waited; so did Dr Browne, a downy bird if ever there was one.

'Mrs Powell did,' said Detective Constable Crosby into the silence.

Sloan groaned inwardly. All the good books on how to question a suspect or a witness suggested that one of the two police officers – and there should always be two – should adopt an aggressive approach and the other one a more softly-softly manner. In practice in almost all cases the person being questioned turned away from the 'nasty' policeman and spoke more openly to the 'nice' one – who would then give every indication that they understood and sympathized. None – but none – of the good books advocated having a half-witted investigating officer with two left feet as the second man.

'If I may say so,' pointed out the doctor, 'the patient is not always in the best position to judge, but . . .'

'But?' Sloan seized on the word. He really would have to have another go at Inspector Harpe about letting Crosby transfer to Traffic Division after all.

'But,' said Browne realistically, 'they usually make a better fist of it than the relatives do.' He regarded the two policemen straightly. 'Now then, gentlemen, what is all this about?'

Detective Inspector Sloan gave the general practitioner a carefully edited résumé of Mrs Powell's allegations.

'She died after a long illness,' said Dr Browne, touching a button on an intercom and asking a receptionist to bring him the late Gertrude Powell's notes, 'but ye'll know that already.'

'Yes, doctor,' said Sloan. Another factor the good books on questioning always stressed was the importance of the interview taking place in surroundings unfamiliar to the subject being questioned. Not, of course, that this implied approval of police-state tactics – such as first leading a bewildered captive up and down through labyrinthine corridors finally to settle in the cellars of the building and thus patently out of earshot of everyone else. Unfortunately, interviewing the doctor in his own consulting room gave him – not the police – the edge.

'And the family had been told,' said Angus Browne. 'I made a point of doing that early on.'

Sloan made a note. Something else the good books stressed as important was the positioning of the interviewee. It wasn't like that here. Crosby had been relegated to the chair reserved for the patient's friend or chaperon – well away from whatever action there was. And he, Sloan, was sitting on the patient's chair, where the full light from the window fell upon his face.

'At least two months ago,' said Browne calmly. It was the doctor's face that was in shadow.

'I see.' Nor was Sloan sitting across a desk but at right angles to the medical man. It was hard to be confrontational – let alone bring pressure to bear – while sitting sideways on. As it happened, he wanted to do neither of these things: but he did very badly want to know everything he could about the life and death of Gertrude Powell.

'Moreover, she was in a uraemic coma at the end,' said Angus Browne briskly, 'and there's no two ways about that.'

'Ah, the end . . .' Sloan began carefully. These days witnesses as well as suspects had to be handled with kid gloves. Not, naturally, that he had ever thought that it was fair to sit a man on a chair in the middle of a room and then circle round him, throwing questions at the man from behind his back so that he was forever spinning round, off-base, to face his interlocutor. 'I wanted to talk to you about the end, doctor.'

'Not unexpected,' said Browne immediately. 'As it happened, I saw her the day she died.'

'You were sent for?'

'I was sent for to see someone else at the Manor and naturally I looked in on her, too.'

'May we ask who it . . .'

'Judge Gillespie,' said Browne. 'He's always been a bit of an old woman about his health. Ye'll notice his Hippocratic facies if you see him.'

'Beg pardon, doctor?'

'Lower jaw hanging open as if he was dead.' He shrugged. 'It's not to be wondered at. He's been very, very shaky since he hit ninety.'

'Like that clock,' said Crosby.

'What clock?' asked the doctor.

'You know,' said Crosby, beginning to chant, 'the one in the song that stood ninety years on the wall, tick tock, and stopped, never to go again, the day the old man died.'

'The Judge hasn't died,' said Dr Browne, regarding the constable in a distinctly clinical way. 'Although I agree some people do die when they've hit a new decade. Dangerous things, birthdays. Make you think. Especially when you're suffering from too many of 'em.'

'So, doctor . . .' resumed Sloan tenaciously.

'The birthday,' carried on the doctor, 'that really worries a lot of men . . .'

'Forty?' suggested Crosby.

'No,' said Dr Browne, recognizing a Freudian slip when he heard one. 'It's the one at the age at which their own fathers died.' The general practitioner pulled open the late Mrs Powell's medical record envelope. 'I get a lot of nervous men in then.'

Detective Inspector Sloan leaned forward, undeterred. 'Mrs Powell . . .'

'It so happens, Inspector,' said the doctor, neatly playing a trump card, 'that I had asked one of the hospital consultants to take a look at her a week or so before she died.'

'You did?' Sloan tried not to sound too interested. He was aiming for what was known as an openended interview. In theory, the semi-structured format allowed respondents to talk at length about any matter that concerned them yet still left the interviewer scope to explore difficult issues. In reality it seemed the doctor was making all the running. 'Do you always do that?'

'No.'

'So why would that have been in this case then?'

'Can't be too careful these days, Inspector.' Browne shrugged. 'It makes for defensive medicine, of course, and that's bad, but it's better than afterwards having people think you could have done more for their nearest and dearest.'

'Would it have been true to say that you wished

you had done so in the case of the late Mrs Maude Chalmers-Hyde?'

'It would have been true to say that in the event, it would have saved there having to be a post-mortem in her case,' conceded Angus Browne, in no whit put out. 'And spared the Matron out there a little concern which ultimately turned out not to have been justified. That's all.'

'Better safe than sorry,' put in Crosby.

'In this case, yes.'

'This other doctor who saw Mrs Powell . . .' persisted Sloan.

'Dr Edwin Beaumont, one of the physicians from the Berebury Hospital Trust,' said Browne, shaking a letter out of the patient's medical record envelope and onto his desk. 'He examined her at my request and confirmed that there was nothing more to be done for Mrs Powell.'

'In writing?'

'Aye, man. In writing.' The bushy eyebrows became even more prominent. 'Ye'll be interested to know that in Beaumont's opinion – and I may say he's a man greatly respected within the profession – as well as in my own, the patient was well beyond aid. That good enough for you?'

Chapter Eight

And plant fresh laurels where they kill

'Very difficult to say at this stage, sir.' Detective Inspector Sloan had next been driven by Detective Constable Crosby to the home of Lionel and Julia Powell on the other side of the county. He was addressing Lionel Powell.

The two policemen might have left Dr Browne's consulting rooms behind at Larking but Sloan anyway had not quite abandoned the medical mode of doling out only such information as was absolutely necessary for his own purposes.

'Later, perhaps, sir.' Indeed, it had occurred to Sloan as he sat in the comfort of the Powells' sitting room that the amount of strictly accurate knowledge given out by the police to anyone involved in an investigation – including the press – was every bit as carefully controlled as that released by a skilled medical practitioner with bad news to impart to a patient.

Knowledge was power all right.

'You will understand, Inspector,' said Lionel

Powell, 'that we need to know where we go from here.'

'You can't just leave things hanging in the air like this, Inspector,' supplemented Julia Powell. 'It's not right.'

'I can assure you we're doing our best, madam.' Sloan supposed the doctor, too, could always utter this comfortable platitude. Both professionals, though, could choose to release news – good and bad – in their own time and that was what mattered. In the handling of a difficult situation timing could be of the essence. Having the timing in one's own hands was power, too.

Lionel Powell underlined his wife's remark. 'Obviously certain matters must be attended to as soon as possible.'

'That is one of the things we are looking into,' murmured Sloan. Dr Browne, he imagined, might say something very similar about the significant result of an X-ray which the doctor already knew and the patient didn't. He, on much the same basis, did know what the immediate outcome of the post-mortem on Mrs Powell, senior, had been, and it was a good deal too inconclusive for his liking.

'My mother-in-law's funeral can't be postponed indefinitely,' said Julia Powell more specifically. 'It isn't seemly.'

'Indeed not, madam,' lied Sloan.

He forbore to say that it could be postponed just as long as the law wished. One thing was certain, anyway, and that was that the deceased wasn't going to be buried until he, Sloan, knew whether or not Gertrude Powell had been murdered, and if so, preferably only after he had found out by whom.

And why.

'And since I'm also one of her executors,' advanced Lionel, 'there are now a number of other circumstances which must be taken into consideration before we can begin the winding up of her financial affairs.' He gave silent thanks that the executors weren't expected to wind up affairs of the heart.

'I do appreciate that, sir.' And Sloan did. He knew that where there was a will, as well as there being a way, there was almost always a relative or two or three. And nothing – but nothing – split heirs like a will. 'But you must remember that we are talking about the possibility of murder . . . your late mother, for one, thought so.'

'Quite, quite,' mumbled Powell, caving in suspiciously soon. 'I didn't mean to . . .'

'So there are one or two facts we should first like to establish about your mother's past,' continued Sloan smoothly.

Lionel Powell stiffened. 'My mother was always very reticent about her early days.'

'Indeed, sir?' The policeman in Sloan was sorry to hear it; the man in him wasn't. Quite a few crimes of passion would have been avoided by a decent reticence on the part of all those concerned.

'Never spoke of them at all,' said the civil servant repressively.

'And you never asked?' put in Detective Constable Crosby. He'd been shown to a stiff chair with a spoonbill back and was getting bored.

'Naturally,' Powell said awkwardly, 'I used to try to get her to tell me about when she was young but she would never talk about later on.'

'Later on?' Sloan seized on this.

'The war,' said Lionel Powell. 'Donald Tulloch – he was her first husband – was killed in action in North Africa. He survived the famous Tinchel at Wadi el Gebra but . . .'

'Tinchel?'

'That was what the Fearnshires called the battle there.' He frowned. 'I believe it's something Scottish to do with a circle of hunters driving deer together by gradually closing in on them.'

Julia Powell gave a shudder. 'How horrid!'

Lionel Powell said, 'The Regiment added it to their battle honours afterwards. It was where the Fearnshires held out against overwhelming odds.'

'Fought to the last man, did they?' asked Crosby, wriggling in his chair in an attempt to make himself more comfortable, and far, far removed in time, distance, experience and imagination from any battlefield.

Powell gave him an odd look. 'Not quite. Donald Tulloch was among those who survived – but he was killed at Tobruk a month or so afterwards.' Powell hurried on, seized by a sudden idea that police resources might be helpful in the matter. 'I always understood from my mother that she had then got married again but we don't know to whom. It was on the rebound, she said, and the marriage didn't last.'

'Funny, that,' remarked Detective Constable Crosby.

'It's a bit of a mystery,' conceded Lionel Powell, 'our not knowing whom she married, that's all.'

The effect of this deliberately low-key exchange was completely undermined by Julia Powell, who said tartly, 'You can say that again.'

'You'd better come to my sitting room,' said Muriel Peden to Sloan and Crosby when they reached Almstone again. She grimaced. 'It's about the only place in the whole Manor that you could call really private.'

'No peace for the wicked . . .' began Crosby.

'That will do very nicely, Matron, thank you,' said Sloan quickly. That would do from Crosby, too . . . wickedness was a matter for careful judgement. He should know by now that the duty of the police was only to establish what had happened and how; whether an action was wicked was something for Parliament – or the parson – to decide.

'And then,' said Sloan, 'perhaps I might see Mrs

Forbes.' Someone here who just wouldn't die must be worth checking on.

'Poor Mrs Forbes,' said the Matron. 'Yes, I really think she'll be the next to go and one cannot be too sorry about that.'

They were soon all ensconced in a room at once cosy and quite stylish. The Matron favoured pale green Dralon upholstery and curtains, the effect considerably enlivened by Kaffe Fassett-coloured cushions. A half-worked tapestry of a design of dusky pink and red roses stood on a frame by her chair, loose ends of wool hanging down from the canvas.

Mrs Peden appeared relieved to be talking to the policemen. 'I'm sorry. I realize now I should have said something straight away . . .'

Sloan said nothing.

She hurried on. 'You see, before it didn't seem terribly important that someone had been in Mrs Powell's room, Inspector, but after what happened at the funeral I thought you ought to know as soon as possible.'

'And how did you yourself know, madam?'

She stirred restlessly in her chair. 'When I went in there at first after she'd died it just struck me that some of her things had been moved about a little. Not very far, you understand, but I'm sure they weren't exactly where they had been, especially a funny little Egyptian ornament she was always very fond of. It was there but it wasn't in its usual place.'

'Go on.'

'I didn't say anything at the time to anyone because I didn't know that anything was missing, you understand.' She searched his face anxiously as if to make sure that he did understand. 'Not then, that is . . .'

'When?' It would be the first thing that Superintendent Leeyes would want to know. That, and why old ladies couldn't die quietly without adding to the workload of F Division of the Calleshire County Constabulary.

'When we first cleared the room. That was after Mrs Powell's son said he had been very much hoping that his late mother's letters would be there.'

'And they weren't?' put in Crosby, who had settled himself very comfortably on the Matron's sofa, plumping up a generous cushion as he did so.

'Not that we could see.' She hesitated. 'Mr Powell said it was quite important. What made it more worrying was that Hazel Finch was sure they had been there before she died.'

'Ah.' Sloan made a note. What made it more worrying for him was that Lionel Powell had made no mention of any missing letters to the police. The letter that the police did know about with its allegations of murder had already been dispatched to Forensic, and a copy and a specimen of Gertrude Powell's handwriting had gone post-haste to a specialist in that arcane subject.

The Matron added, 'In an old chocolate box.'

Detective Inspector Christopher Dennis Sloan, much-married man, made another note. Some things never changed. He knew that, foolishly sentimental or not, his own wife, Margaret, kept his letters to her in the very first chocolate box he had given her. Right at the far back of a locked drawer. 'Tied up in pink ribbon?' he asked.

'No.' She smiled faintly. 'But with a picture of roses on the lid. Hazel said the box had always been kept just inside the top drawer of her dressing table.'

'I take it that Mrs Powell wouldn't have been able to get to them to destroy them herself?'

'Oh no, Inspector. She was unconscious for several days before she died.'

'And she hadn't asked anyone else to burn them unread after she'd gone?' Too deep for words was his own wife's illogical conviction that the only person in the whole world who must never read their love letters to each other was their own son.

'Hazel says not her, anyway. And,' the Matron chose her words with obvious care, 'I've always found her a very truthful girl.'

Detective Inspector Sloan nodded. 'The other staff?'

'Hadn't been in there at all after Mrs Powell died,' said the Matron promptly. 'I don't, of course, know about before.'

'But afterwards?'

'I locked the door of her room myself while we were waiting for the undertakers.'

87

'The keys?'

'Hanging in the office.'

Sloan sighed. 'How accessible?'

'Very, I'm afraid, Inspector. You must remember that this is meant to be a home from home, not a prisoner of war camp,' she gave a tolerant smile, 'for all that the residents do have what they call an Escape Committee.'

'Me, I don't blame them.' Crosby hitched himself up on the sofa cushions and looked round. 'Well, they are here for the duration, aren't they?'

'The Escape Committee is for arranging outings and excursions,' protested Mrs Peden feebly. 'To the theatre and open gardens in the summer and so forth.'

Detective Constable Crosby, occasional reader of war stories, said, 'Got a Senior British Officer, then, have they?'

'The Brigadier,' said the Matron.

Sloan looked up. 'Not the Judge?'

'Too old,' she said, adding lightly, 'besides, judges don't make leaders, do they?'

Sloan looked at her plump and kindly features with new eyes. An unlikely spiritual sister of Superintendent Leeyes, she, too, had spotted a judicial weakness. Terrier-like, he returned to the matter of the keys.

'Each on its own named hook, Inspector,' she said. 'It has to be that way because we don't let the residents bolt themselves in their rooms in case they need help.'

Detective Constable Crosby suddenly stirred again. 'Where was the ornament?'

'On the windowsill,' said Mrs Peden. 'That's where it always was.'

'And where is it now?' asked Sloan more pertinently.

'In our little library here, Inspector. Mr Powell presented it to us here in his mother's memory when he took all Mrs Powell's other things away with him the day she died.'

'Except her letters,' remarked Crosby.

'Except her letters,' agreed the Matron.

Chapter Nine

But their strong nerves at last must yield

Matron's knock on Mrs Forbes' bedroom door was so perfunctory that Detective Inspector Sloan knew that she was not expecting to hear any response from its occupant.

Lying in the bed and curled up in what the medical professionals called the foetal position was a figure almost as unaware as a newborn baby of anything other than its attendants and food and warmth. Lending a touch of verisimilitude to this neo-natal comparison, a baby's feeding bottle was tucked in the bedclothes alongside her.

Muriel Peden advanced on the patient with a Florence Nightingale brightness. 'Hullo, Mrs Forbes, I've brought along a gentleman who just wants to make sure you're all right.'

Detective Inspector Sloan regarded the woman with unwonted compassion as he saw the effort it cost her to speak. Gnarled hands clenched with pain as her head inched up slowly to try to look at him.

'Yes, thank you,' Elizabeth Forbes enunciated carefully. 'Quite all right.'

All Sloan could think of was something that Rudyard Kipling had written and a chorus line at that. 'No one thinks of winter when the grass is green!' This was Mrs Forbes' winter, all right . . . and a long, long one.

As soon as she had finished speaking her head started to descend again towards her chest until her chin came to rest on her breastbone.

Kipling had been writing about Napoleon on St Helena but 'If you've taken the first step, you will take the last!' applied just as well to Elizabeth Forbes ending her days at the Manor.

Muriel Peden expertly slid the feeding bottle up between Mrs Forbes' fingers and, like a blind nursling, the old lady immediately brought it up to her mouth and started to suck.

'How long has she been like this?' Sloan asked the Matron in a low voice. What Kipling had written was, 'After open weather you may look for snow!' He found himself hoping that Mrs Forbes had had her full mede of open weather.

'A long time,' said Mrs Peden.

Sloan nodded. With Napoleon Bonaparte it had been, 'What you cannot finish you must leave undone.' If Elizabeth Forbes had left anything undone, it was too late now to do it.

'She came in here after her husband died,' murmured the Matron.

An involuntary spasm of pity crossed Sloan's face – for Mrs Forbes, not for Napoleon, who had been the architect of his own troubles.

Matron said, 'He'd looked after her for as long as he could up until then. And he was getting old and frail, too.'

'Of course,' said Sloan. Kipling had put his finger on it all right with his, 'Morning never tries you till the afternoon.'

'And she had no one else, you see.'

'No family, you mean?'

'That's right. She's quite alone in the world, Inspector.'

It was Dr Samuel Johnson who came into Sloan's mind as they left the room. An essay he'd been set long ago on something the Great Cham had said: '"Pity is an acquired emotion" – Discuss.' The policeman in Sloan reasserted itself before his mind could run on any further.

In this setting having no immediate heirs could be a positive safeguard.

On the other hand it might not.

The most secure telephone at the Manor was in a cupboard under the stairs. It was cramped and dark there but at least it had the merit of being private. This was just as well, because Superintendent Leeyes did not mince his words.

'That judge you asked about, Sloan . . .'

'Yes, sir?' Sloan positioned his notebook at the ready.

'Nothing known against. Got a mysterious gong after the war – a Military Order of the British Empire – for unspecified services rendered while in the Judge Advocate's Department.'

Shakespeare's play *Othello* was not a good one for schoolboys – perhaps it would have been more of an education for girls, Sloan didn't know – but he had never forgotten the Moor's, 'I have done the State some service, and they know't.'

'Then,' said Leeyes, 'he became a Recorder over at Calleford.' The Superintendent sniffed. 'Quite highly thought of, I understand, in those days. Things were different then, of course.'

'Quite so,' said Sloan hastily. He already knew Leeyes' 'good old days' speech almost by heart now. Hanging and flogging came into nearly every sentence.

'He's probably lost his Elgins at his age, though, Sloan, so watch it.'

'Yes, sir,' promised Sloan.

'Now, did you get anywhere with that general practitioner over at Larking?'

'I think, sir,' replied Detective Inspector Sloan, conscious of theological overtones learned at his mother's knee, 'you could say that earlier he had had doubts.'

'Doubts?' echoed Superintendent Leeyes, never a man troubled by lack of conviction.

'We have reason to believe he'd suspected something amiss over another death at the Manor.'

'And why,' enquired Leeyes at his most magisterial, 'didn't Browne tell us that?'

'Because Dr Dabbe couldn't find anything wrong.' Sloan coughed. 'Even so, I'm going to get Crosby to make a list of all the deaths at the Manor in the last few years.'

'Dabbe's only a doctor,' snorted Leeyes. 'He's not infallible.'

'No, sir,' agreed Sloan. 'I know that.'

Any Temple of Truth, he knew, was only as good as its current custodian. 'But I think it might explain why Dr Browne was especially careful over Gertude Powell's death.'

'So I should hope,' said Leeyes robustly.

'Dr Browne even brought a medical consultant out from Berebury to make sure that nothing more could be done.'

'Needed his hand holding, did he?'

'Not necessarily.'

'Covering his back, then?'

'Taking precautions,' said Sloan. 'He's a pretty wily bloke.'

'It's downright unnatural, if you ask me,' pronounced the Superintendent. 'I mean, everyone there's knocking on a bit, aren't they?'

Sloan decided in the interests of his future pension to let this gross slur on the medical profession pass and concentrate instead on the police implications. 'I don't think it was the knocking-on aspect, sir, that troubled Dr Browne so much as the – er – knocking off.'

'That, Sloan,' said Leeyes icily, 'if you remember, was what was bothering the deceased, too. You'd better get moving.'

Getting moving, Sloan decided, certainly ought to include another chat with Hazel Finch, the care assistant.

They found her sitting at the kitchen table taking the weight off her feet, a large mug of tea in front of her. Without speaking, the cook, Lisa Haines, put two more mugs on the table and reached for the teapot.

'We just need a little more background,' said Sloan persuasively, pulling up a chair beside them, 'and then we'll be on our way.'

'That's all very well, Inspector,' objected Lisa Haines, 'but what's going to happen about poor Mrs Powell's funeral? You can't just take her away like that and nothing said. It's not right.'

'Out of our hands, Mrs Haines.' Detective Inspector Sloan looked as solemn as he knew how. 'It's up to the Coroner now.'

'I'd forgotten all about him,' said the cook, who had actually never given that august personage a single thought. 'There now . . .'

'The Coroner has the last word about any death,'

said Sloan. He himself almost always found any mention of the holder of that mysterious office of the Crown helpful. The exception was when his name cropped up in the presence of the Coroner's arch-enemy, Superintendent Leeyes.

'I suppose someone's got to,' she said doubtfully. In the Manor, it was the Matron who had the last word.

'Yes, indeed,' said Sloan, turning to the care assistant. 'Now, Hazel, if you could just tell me about Mrs Powell's box of letters that isn't there, I promise we'll soon be on our way.'

Unperturbed, Hazel Finch confirmed everything the Matron had told Sloan.

'And could you describe for us, too, the ornament that was moved?'

'Funny-looking thing,' said Hazel. 'Egyptian, she always said it was. 'Bout so high.' She lifted a pudgy hand almost a foot above the kitchen table. 'But not very wide.'

'What was it made of?'

'That I don't rightly know. China, I think, because Mrs Powell was always on about me not breaking it.' She patted the vast glazed-pottery teapot on the table. 'It was shiny, like this.'

'Colour?'

Hazel Finch screwed up her eyes in the effort of recollection. 'Sort of greeny-blue.'

'And what did it look like?'

This was clearly even more of a challenge but

after a moment or two the care assistant said, frowning, 'A sort of keyhole with arms but with the key left in the wrong way. You know, pointing upwards instead of through.'

Detective Constable Crosby looked up. 'Did she call it Keyhole Kate?'

'I didn't think nothing of it myself,' said Hazel, ignoring the interruption, 'but Mrs Powell set a lot of store by having it where she could see it. Always kep' it on the corner of her dressing table.'

Crosby drained his mug. 'A mascot then?' he suggested. 'Seeing as it wasn't very nice to look at.'

'She said it had brought her luck,' agreed Hazel, 'though, me, I didn't see that being ill and in bed here was luck.'

'Good beds, good company and good food,' countered the cook, who was older and wiser. 'Let me tell you, Hazel Finch, there's plenty of old ladies what'd be glad of all three.'

'You've both been very helpful,' said Sloan. This was quite true. If nothing more, Hazel Finch had shown she would make a good witness. The Crown Prosecution Service liked a good witness. He shut his notebook with rather more vigour than was absolutely necessary and ostentatiously put his pen away inside his jacket. 'Tell me,' he said conversationally, 'what was it that so upset the Judge on his birthday?'

'His birthday present,' said Hazel promptly.

'Ah . . .' That took Sloan straight back to a certain

birthday when a young Christopher Dennis Sloan had dearly wanted a bicycle and got a pair of football boots instead. He had been disappointed but not surprised. With the ruthless calculation of child-hood, he'd soon worked out that his school would have insisted on the football boots but not the bicycle. In Sloan's day bicycles were optional.

Crosby's mind was working along quite different lines. 'What on earth could an old geezer of ninety want for his birthday?'

'Don't ask me,' said Hazel Finch. 'All I can tell you is what he got.'

'And that was?' asked Sloan.

'His old coat repaired.'

'And cleaned,' put in Lisa Haines.

'His coat?' echoed Sloan.

'He had one of those great big army overcoats,' said the cook.

'A British Warm,' decided Crosby. 'I've seen pic-tures of them.'

'A greatcoat, he called it,' said Hazel.

Lisa Haines spotted Crosby's empty mug and automatically reached for the teapot. 'Whatever it was called, it was in a terrible state. Practically falling to pieces.'

'He wouldn't throw it away for all that it was in rags and tatters,' said the care assistant. 'He wouldn't ever let me send it to the cleaners, either.' She took a long draught of tea. 'And that wasn't for want of trying.' She smiled benevolently at the two police-men. 'Mind you, some old gentlemen get like that.'

'I'm sure,' said Sloan. He saw the ragged and tattered regularly under the railway arches by Bere-bury Station. But they were poor. The Judge presumably wasn't.

'So for his birthday some of the residents decided to have it cleaned and mended – well, to mend it themselves, actually,' Lisa Haines said. 'More tea, Inspector?'

'And proper put out he was, I can tell you,' said Hazel Finch stoutly, 'when the Judge saw what they'd done to it.'

'So shaky he couldn't barely get his glass up to his mouth without spilling it,' contributed the cook.

'You'd've thought he'd've been grateful,' said Hazel. 'Wouldn't you?'

'But he wasn't?' said the policeman.

Hazel shook her head. 'He was very upset.'

'Frightened, more like,' said Lisa Haines soberly. 'But we never did know why.'

Chapter Ten

They tame but one another still

To describe a gathering of four geriatric patients in a care home as a council of war might at first sight have seemed to be stretching a point: especially when the group comprised an old lady visibly a victim of osteoarthritis and three old men, one of whom was in a wheelchair. And yet it would have been difficult to dismiss the little meeting in the Bridge Room of the Manor as anything else.

Miss Bentley tapped the floor with her walking stick and the others stopped talking at once. 'Now,' she said peremptorily, 'will someone kindly tell me exactly what has been going on?'

'We don't know,' said Captain Markyate.

'Can't understand it at all,' said Hamish MacIver. The spick and span former Military Person of the morning had gone. Now he just looked a tired old man.

'Who on earth would have wanted to kill Gertie?' asked Walter Bryant of no one in particular. 'She'd been dying for ages anyway.'

'Her son?' suggested Peter Markyate, taking this literally. 'Well,' he said, looking round, 'presumably he gets all her money.'

The Brigadier tugged his moustache. 'Dammit, the fellow hardly ever visited his mother.'

'And never stayed very long when he did, either,' sniffed Markyate. 'He usually said he had to leave pretty soon because of his wife.'

'As well he might.' Walter Bryant leaned forward. 'He always left Julia in the car park if she came with him. I know because I used to see her waiting there while I was waiting for Miss Ritchie to come and take me for a run.'

Hamish MacIver muttered under his breath, 'Take you for a ride, you mean.'

'Now, Hamish . . .' Bryant bristled.

'Sorry,' apologized the Brigadier gruffly.

'So when he did come to see his mother,' said Peter Markyate, 'he was alone with her.'

'What are you getting at, Peter?' asked the Brigadier.

'You only need one opportunity to kill,' said Walter Bryant, eagerly edging his electric wheelchair forward. 'I remember when A Company first came under fire at Wadi el Gebra and . . .'

'Walter,' Miss Bentley gave an exasperated snort, 'I don't think what you did at Wadi el Gebra has a lot of bearing on what we're talking about today.'

It was the Brigadier who flushed while Markyate intervened. 'Steady on,' he said earnestly. 'We couldn't have managed there without old Walter. Those terrible German tanks . . .'

Miss Bentley ruthlessly cut this military reminiscence short. 'That's not the point. What I want to know is why Gertie thought she was going to be murdered.' She searched the faces of the others carefully. 'What exactly made her think that?'

'That's what we don't know,' said the Brigadier. 'That's the trouble.'

Miss Bentley looked round. 'Didn't she tell anyone?'

'Not us, anyway,' declared MacIver.

'Not Matron, either,' said Markyate, 'because I asked her.'

'That I can believe,' said Miss Bentley trenchantly, 'because Matron would have done something straight away.'

They all nodded. On this they were agreed. Matron was a woman of action.

MacIver said, 'Believe you me, Hetty, we're as perplexed as everyone else.'

'Hmm,' said Miss Bentley, wearing a facial expression which over the years had withered staff, parents and pupils alike. 'It isn't,' she remarked thoughtfully, 'as if Gertie had held with all this medical business of Living Wills. You know, signing statements when you're fit and well that you don't want to be revived if you're ever so ill that your quality of life has gone.'

Peter Markyate said, 'She wasn't ever one to hand decisions over to anyone else. Not Gertie.'

'And definitely not to doctors,' said Bryant.

'Rather not.' Captain Markyate endorsed this immediately. 'And she told 'em so at the hospital, too. Don't you remember how she got quite upset when some whippersnapper of a house physician asked her if she wanted to be resuscitated if she collapsed in there. Life was always worth living, she said. Gave them her curtain lecture on the importance of enjoying life to the full.'

'And to the bitter end,' said Bryant.

'One of her favourite sayings, if you remember,' said Hamish MacIver, 'was that life was quite short enough as it was.'

'And that one about "the best was yet to be",' said Markyate gruffly. 'Remember?'

'She wasn't riddled with arthritis,' said Miss Bentley feelingly.

'Gertie always seemed quite content with things as they were,' murmured Markyate. 'That was one of the best things about her.'

The Brigadier said, 'She wouldn't ever become a member of the Escape Committee.'

'Not ever,' agreed Markyate. 'I mean,' he added, flustered, 'she hadn't joined and then changed her mind, if you know what I mean. Some people,' he bumbled on, 'do.'

'I can understand that,' volunteered Walter Bryant, looking a little embarrassed. 'Take myself, for instance. Knowing Margot Ritchie has wrought a big change in the way I now see things . . . I'm resigning with immediate effect.'

Miss Bentley looked as if she was about to speak but then thought better of it.

'I'm thinking very differently these days,' he went on earnestly, 'about almost everything.'

'Circumstances alter cases,' said the Brigadier diplomatically.

'Hmm,' said Miss Bentley again.

'Elizabeth Forbes just changed her mind,' put in Peter Markyate, 'between one day and the next.'

'Don't know why, I'm sure,' said the Brigadier. 'It's all right for old Walter here, but any change in circumstances there, poor woman, was for the worse surely.'

Walter Bryant looked shrewdly across at him. 'And what about Maisie Carruthers, Hamish? Will she join now she's here, do you think? Or doesn't she believe in our Escape Committee and the Almstone Pragmatic Sanction?'

The Brigadier stiffened visibly, his face turning a turkey-red. 'I really have no idea at all,' he said distantly. 'You'll have to ask her that yourselves. I'm keeping out of it.'

In Sloan's book 'getting moving' also included interviewing Judge Calum Gillespie. That aged legal gentleman received Detective Inspector Sloan and

Detective Constable Crosby in his room at the Manor with an old-fashioned courtesy.

'Is this a duty visit, officers,' he enquired, 'or may I offer you both a glass of Madeira? I've got some very passable Old Trinity House Bual here if you would like it.'

'Duty, I'm afraid, sir,' said Sloan. He knew full well that in the Judge's private world officers and gentlemen and just plain officers were two quite different categories of men.

'Pity. You will, I trust, not think me uncivil if I myself indulge?'

'Indeed not,' said Sloan truthfully. If there was one Latin tag fully appreciated by every policeman it was *in vino veritas*.

'At my time of life a little alcohol helps keep the arteries open.' Judge Gillespie tottered to a side table and unstoppered a cut-glass decanter. Sloan watched as the neck of the decanter danced dangerously over the sherry glass. Miraculously, though, it never actually touched it and equally marvellously the Judge carried the full glass back without actually spilling it. He sat down and took a sip, saying, 'Ah, that's better. Now, settle down and tell me why you've come to see me. I don't get many visitors from the – ah – outside world these days.'

'We have reason to believe that the late Mrs Powell,' began Sloan without preamble, 'thought she was being murdered.'

'And does anyone else think so?' Two bright bird-like eyes regarded the two policemen with lively interest.

'No one whom we know about,' said Sloan with care.

'And was she?' The Judge turned his head to one side quizzically. 'Murdered, I mean.'

'We don't know yet.' Sloan saw no reason for prevarication. The Judge might have got a tremor but he still seemed to have all his marbles as well.

'Ah . . .' Calum Gillespie took another appreciative sip of the Bual before using two hands to lower the glass onto an occasional table. 'Would it be – er – presumptuous of me to enquire whether you, too, have grounds for thinking she might have been?'

'Not, sir, what you could call really firm evidence,' replied Sloan, giving him full marks for getting straight to the heart of the matter. 'Not yet.'

'I see.' The Judge drew his eyebrows together in a prodigious frown and became sunk in thought. 'Difficult for you . . . for everybody.'

Detective Inspector Sloan, experienced giver of evidence, waited much as he would have done – did – in court. Judges always took as long as they needed – as long as they wanted – to think. It was one of their privileges. It was not for them to be harried into ill-considered speech by counsel or trapped into the all too revealing 'response immediate'.

'And would I be right,' the old man said at long last, 'in concluding therefore that the result of any post-mortem examination has so far been inconclusive?'

'Awaiting the full report,' said Sloan ambiguously. Not only had the old boy got all his marbles but they were patently in excellent working order.

'Why, then, Inspector, might I ask, have you come to see me?'

'For background,' said Sloan glibly. Too glibly, because Crosby seemed to think that the word needed amplification.

The constable looked earnestly at the frail old man and said in loud tones, 'We want to know, sir, if there's been any dirty work at the crossroads that you know about here at the Manor.'

'There's always been dirty work at the crossroads, Constable,' the Judge said unexpectedly.

Crosby said, 'I know but . . .'

'Because the crossroads were always where they had the gibbet,' said Calum Gillespie hortatively, reaching for his glass of Madeira.

'I didn't mean then,' protested Crosby. 'I meant now.'

'And they had it there,' went on the nonagenarian, serenely disregarding the detective constable's remarks, 'because the crossroads were usually where the parish boundaries met and they always had the gibbet on the boundary if they could . . . saved having two and kept it out of your own backyard.'

'Quite so,' Detective Inspector Sloan came in smoothly, reminding himself that in the early days of this Judge they had hanged men. And women. What Crosby needed was hanging out to dry. He leaned forward and said, 'I wonder, sir, if you would care to tell us why you are so very attached to your old coat?'

The glass that had so nearly reached Judge Calum Gillespie's lips fell suddenly out of his nerveless hands, sending its delectable contents spilling out stickily over the old man's suit.

'Why have you come?' he quavered breathlessly, his face turning an unhealthy shade of purple. 'Who sent you here?'

Chapter Eleven

Early or late
They stoop to fate

'Then what happened?' Superintendent Leeyes
wanted to know. As was always his wont, he was
sitting comfortably in the relative calm of his own
office.

'He rolled over and played dead,' said Detective
Inspector Sloan, who was standing uneasily at the
other side of the Superintendent's desk. He and
Crosby had got back to Berebury Police Station at
long last only to find Leeyes ready and waiting,
spider-like, to rush out and ensnare them in his web.
'For all that he'd been a judge in his day.'

'Which he wasn't, I take it?' Leeyes said. 'Dead,
I mean.'

'No, sir,' said Sloan. 'Far from it, in fact.'

'Alive and kicking,' contributed Crosby.

'Oh, we whistled up a couple of care staff pretty
quickly,' said Sloan, 'and they brisked about a bit.
Got him cleaned up and so forth and then into bed,
but . . .'

'But he wouldn't talk to us at all after that, sir,' put in the detective constable. 'Couldn't get a dicky bird out of him for love nor money.'

'And we can't make him talk,' said Leeyes more than a little wistfully. Some of the more liberal provisions of the new Police and Criminal Evidence Act had not gone down at all well with the Superintendent of F Division of the Calleshire County Constabulary.

'No, sir,' replied Sloan rather more firmly than perhaps he should have done. 'We can't.'

'Was he mute of malice?' enquired Leeyes with interest. 'We might get him for that.'

'More like mute of enlightened self-interest,' said Sloan, who had himself picked something up from the class the Superintendent had once attended on 'The Whig Supremacy'.

Leeyes glared at his two subordinates, the reference now quite lost upon him. 'So what exactly is going on out there?'

'Something, I'm sure,' said Sloan fairly, before Crosby could speak, 'but we don't know exactly what. Yet.'

'Well, you'd better find out pretty quickly,' said Leeyes, 'because we'll have old Locombe-Stableford on our backs in no time at all. To say nothing,' he added gloomily, 'of the press. I can see the headlines now.'

So unfortunately could Sloan. And you couldn't get anything cornier than 'Mystery at the Manor'. Or

'Who Moved Mysterious Figure in the Bedroom?' Bedrooms always made good headlines. Figures in bedrooms, even better.

Leeyes shuffled some papers about on his desk. 'All I can say, Sloan, is if the pathologist can't come up with the answer, then you'll have to.'

'I don't know about the deceased and her last letter, sir,' he said, ignoring this, 'but my own feeling is that Judge Gillespie knew exactly what he was doing when he dropped his sherry glass and started playing dumb crambo with us.'

'It seems to me,' pronounced Leeyes crustily, 'that the only people out there who don't seem to know what they are doing are you and Crosby here.'

Crosby took this literally. 'Could be, sir. All the others seem to be sticking together. After all, they or their husbands were all in the same regiment together.'

'And,' pounced Leeyes, 'I suppose that any minute now one of you is going to tell me that everyone in the place has been trained to kill silently and without trace as well.'

Sloan was only half listening. His mind was already running through all that would have to be done the next day. Like those who had buried Sir John Moore at Corunna, he too could only bitterly think of the morrow.

'All the men, anyway,' he responded absently.

*

The coming of Saturday morning had created something of a dilemma for Mrs Maisie Carruthers. On the one hand she itched to appear at breakfast and glean the very latest news. On the other hand her son, Ned, didn't work on Saturdays and he had promised to come to see her as soon as he could. And on one thing she was quite determined and that was to receive him whilst she was still in her bed. He need never know about her debut in the dining room the day before.

Oblique questioning of Hazel Finch when she brought up her breakfast tray had got Maisie little further than learning that the police had finally left the Manor after talking to the Judge and just before the evening meal.

'I thought we'd never get him undressed,' lamented Hazel, 'he was so all to pieces. I don't know what those two policemen had said to him, I'm sure. Not that you'll know the Judge, Mrs Carruthers, being as how you only arrived here yesterday.'

'Known him for years,' said Mrs Carruthers laconically.

'Well, I never,' said Hazel.

'Fine figure of a man he was, too, then.' She gave a reminiscent smile. 'In the war.'

'Uniform always does something for a man, doesn't it?' said Hazel wistfully. 'Now, that young policeman who came here yesterday. He'd have been the better for being in uniform.'

'I dare say,' said Maisie, 'though I'm not sure how he would have looked in a kilt.'

'You don't think of policemen having knees, somehow,' said Hazel, 'do you?'

'Some of them wore shorts. That was when they were in North Africa,' said Mrs Carruthers, looking back in her mind's eye over half a century. She sighed. 'A handsome lot they all were, too. The Judge, the Brigadier, Mr Bryant, even,' she added thoughtfully, 'Captain Markyate and look at them now . . .'

'Poor Captain Markyate. He was in ever such a state last night, too,' volunteered Hazel.

Maisie Carruthers sat up suddenly. 'Had the police . . .'

'It was Friday, you see.'

'Friday?'

'The grace,' said the care assistant. 'We – they – always have the regimental grace said at dinner on Friday evenings.'

'I think I remember it from the old days . . .' began Maisie. In fact the only grace she actually remembered had been the rude soldiery chanting 'Rub-a-dub-dub, thank God for our grub' outside the cookhouse door.

'The Judge usually says it but he wasn't up to it last night and so Captain Markyate had to step in.'

'Why not the Brigadier?' she asked curiously. 'Surely he's more senior?'

But this Hazel did not know.

'And what,' Maisie led her on cunningly, 'is going to happen now about Mrs Powell's funeral?'

'Don't know,' confessed Hazel. 'The undertaker – young Mr Morton – ever such a polite man he is, Mrs Carruthers, he was on the phone to Matron first thing saying it's never happened to his firm before and how sorry he is about it all.'

'I'm sure he is,' said Maisie Carruthers astringently.

'But he doesn't seem to know anything more than anyone else. I reckon,' she added with unconsciously cold-blooded realism, 'he'll soon be out here anyway for Mrs Forbes.'

Mrs Carruthers sat up alertly. 'Is she a member of the Escape Committee then?'

'I wouldn't know about that,' said the care assistant incuriously, 'but she's going downhill fast and you can't be sorry . . . especially when she's got nobody.'

'Her husband went into the bag at Tobruk,' said Mrs Carruthers. 'He was a prisoner of war for years.'

'What about your husband?' asked Hazel tentatively.

'He was lucky,' said the old lady. 'He got out of the Tinchel at Wadi el Gebra with only a wounded knee. He limped for ever afterwards.'

The care assistant seized on something she understood. 'That was a pity for him, wasn't it? Having to choose between shorts and a kilt with a

114

bad knee. Now, don't you go and let your toast get cold . . .'

'How can I help you?' Hilary Collins was the Deputy Curator of the Greatorex Museum, which was the reason why she and not the Curator himself was on duty in the museum on Saturday mornings.

Detective Inspector Sloan laid an object in a polythene bag on the desk before her.

The young woman regarded it with academic detachment and repeated her question.

Detective Constable Crosby stirred. 'Well, for starters, miss, is it animal, vegetable or mineral?'

'Mineral,' she said, shooting an odd look in his direction.

She, thought Sloan, would have been a good person to have had with them at the Manor the previous evening when they had tracked the green ornament down in the library there. This was not so much a room of books as a regimental museum. Mrs Powell's ornamental piece had joined a bizarre collection of trophies of war and blood sports.

'Glazed composition, actually,' said Hilary Collins, taking off her glasses for a closer look.

'I see,' said Sloan. This was why it hadn't really fitted in among the other memorabilia – which were chiefly fur and feather – of the Fearnshires. It had certainly looked out of place where it was – sitting between some ancient and very tattered bagpipes and a Scottish wild cat, itself a triumph of the art of taxidermy, which was stretched out along the top of a bookcase.

'It's an amulet,' said Hilary Collins.

'And what might an amulet be, miss?' he asked. His question owed nothing to his police training and everything to his childhood. The precept 'If you don't ask, you'll never know' had been ground into him early on. The extra adjuration 'Don't guess because that shows two things you don't know' had come at school later.

'An ancient good-luck charm,' the Deputy Curator informed him.

Crosby uttered a sound that might have been a snort.

'What else can you tell us about it, miss?' said Sloan before the constable could say anything about the quality of luck that had attended Gertie Powell. He himself would have liked to have known a little more about some of the other artefacts in the Manor library. Claymores, dirks and skean-dhus adorned the wall alongside the antlers of long-deceased stags and vulpine heads. After ten minutes in the room he had not been at all sure that former members of the Fearnshires had distinguished between war and blood sports. Under one pointed vulpine mask were the words 'Foxhole – Wadi el Gebra, 1942'.

'Anything that you can tell us, miss, would be helpful.'

'It's not my field, I'm afraid,' warned the young woman, 'so I can only give you very rough details . . .'

'If you would,' said Sloan courteously. That it wasn't your province was something you weren't allowed to say in the Force. Even the War Duties Officer had to be able to direct traffic, arrest a burglar and hold a shield in a Riot Squad. So, in theory, did the Chief Constable, but he was less likely to be put to the test on account of usually being away sitting on a committee somewhere.

'I would say the provenance was almost certainly Egyptian,' she began cautiously.

There had been no doubt about where the stuffed capercaillie standing in the library fireplace had come from. Even Sloan knew that such birds were peculiarly Scottish. Haughty even in death, its beady eyes had – like those of the subject of a portrait whose sitter had looked at the painter while he was working – seemed to follow the two policemen round the room.

'And that it's meant to be symbolic of life,' continued Miss Collins studiously.

This time Crosby's snort was unmistakable.

'Ah . . .' Sloan hadn't needed anyone to explain to him the symbolism of the old sporrans on display in the library. You didn't need to be an anthropologist to know what they and their fine tassels represented. What he'd have liked was a quick refreshing look at Sir James Frazer's book *The Golden Bough*. When he had been a young constable his old

Station Sergeant had always kept a copy by him to remind him that quirks of human behaviour were not confined to the Charge Room of one police station in the county of Calleshire. 'The expurgated version, lad,' he would say to a callow and uncomprehending Sloan. 'Can't go too far. Not in here.'

'It is also meant to stand for dominion,' expounded Hilary Collins, 'although in precisely what way it achieves this, I cannot say.'

Detective Inspector Sloan made a careful note, while uttering a silent prayer that no one would want to take up with him the deep philosophical question of whether there was a link between luck and dominion. Psychiatrists could make something of anything. Or something of nothing. Or even everything of anything.

'The ankh part there,' the Deputy Curator pointed to the outer part, 'that's the loop above the horizontal bar – is an ansate cross . . .'

'The bit like a lacrosse stick with knobs on, you mean?' said Crosby more colloquially.

' . . . and is the symbol of life,' she said hortatively, 'whilst this straight length up the middle here,' she indicated the inside of the loop, 'is the sceptre set in it, which, as you will know, represents power and authority.'

Detective Constable Crosby, who had to make do with a rather grubby warrant card as the symbol of his power and authority, leaned over and took a better look.

'And the date, miss?' asked Sloan. 'How old is it?'

'I'm no expert,' she said self-deprecatingly, 'but I should say something in the region of three thousand years.'

Sloan stared at a piece of work crafted by the hand of man that had lasted longer than anything else he had ever known, his imagination soaring far away beyond the present and mundane. It was his detective constable who brought him back to earth.

'What's it worth?' asked Crosby.

'We're not allowed to give valuations,' said Miss Collins a little primly. 'I think I might say, though, that it would be considered eminently collectable.'

Sloan gave an untroubled nod. For his money, Lionel Powell wouldn't have given it away if he had known it was valuable. Unless, of course, it had held unhappy associations. He'd seen that happen to plenty of things after a death.

The Deputy Curator pointed to the polythene bag. 'If I might be allowed to feel the object, Inspector, I might just be able to tell you some more about it. It's clearly a very interesting piece . . .'

'You've told us all we need to know, miss. Thank you,' said Sloan untruthfully.

As far as Detective Inspector Sloan was concerned, the one interesting thing about the artefact was something that they hadn't mentioned at the museum at all and on which the Deputy Curator was unlikely to be able to give an opinion, this being most definitely not her field. That was that the only fingerprints on it were those of the Matron and of Hazel Finch, who had borne it from the bedroom down to the library at the Manor after Mrs Powell had died.

Before that it had been wiped absolutely clean.

Chapter Twelve

And must give up their murmuring breath

Unlike Maisie Carruthers but with equally careful forethought, Walter Bryant had chosen not to receive his two daughters in the privacy of his own room at the Manor. Instead, he had elected the relatively public setting of the library. Picking your ground was an important military maxim.

Agnes, the elder, kissed him dutifully on the forehead.

He wriggled uncomfortably, mentally chalking up yet another shortcoming to life in a wheelchair. Most – but not all – kisses landed, perforce, on his balding pate.

'Nice to see you, Da,' she said. 'Mike's sorry he couldn't come.'

'Didn't ask him,' growled her father.

'Because it's a Saturday,' she said, ignoring, like her mother before her, what she didn't like, 'he's taken the children to watch the Probables play the Possibles.'

Helen, the younger, sat down opposite him, and

decided not to mention her husband. Her father had never liked him.

'You're not ill, are you, Da, sending for us both like this?' she asked.

'On the contrary,' he said, sitting up very straight. 'I'm feeling fitter than I've done for a long time.'

His daughters exchanged glances.

'Good,' said Helen nervously.

'Much fitter,' he said.

'Splendid,' said Agnes insincerely.

'In fact that's got a lot to do with my news . . . my good news.'

'Good news?' Helen fought to keep the quaver out of her voice. One of the reasons why her father had never liked her husband was his charming – but total – improvidence.

'I've asked Miss Ritchie – Margot – to marry me,' he said. He paused for effect. 'And she said she would.'

'I'll bet she did,' exploded Agnes.

'Oh, dear,' moaned Helen quietly. The only thing that had made her husband's charming improvidence bearable was the thought that one day – in due course, naturally – her half-share – she didn't grudge the other half-share to her sister – of her father's money would come to her. She did grudge it to Miss Margot Ritchie.

'That woman – ' began Agnes. But, catching sight of her father's expression, she thought better of carrying on.

'But what can she offer you?' asked Helen.

'A home,' said Walter Bryant simply.

'But you like it here, Da,' wailed Agnes. Her Mike was a better provider than Helen's husband but there were the boys to be settled and – one day in the future – she was sure she didn't wish her father ill in any way – a few luxuries wouldn't have come amiss. 'You've always said how you've liked the Manor.'

'It's not the same as a home of one's own,' he said.

That silenced both women. Neither had ever offered him a home with them when their mother had died.

'Besides, I think I'll be better off in Miss Ritchie's bungalow,' he said complacently.

Agnes suddenly became very earnest while Helen, more disturbed by the news, started pacing up and down the library behind him.

'But Da,' said Agnes, leaning forward and patting his hand, 'what about your bad heart?'

'It'll stay the same as it's always been. It's my address I'm changing,' he snapped, 'not my vital organs.'

Agnes, who would have liked to have said something further about his vital organs, decided to keep the word 'satyriasis' until she got home. She settled instead for a few pointed remarks about old age.

Her father listened with half an ear. He was attempting to keep his eye on Helen, still distractedly pacing about the library. He tried to spin his wheelchair round to keep her in view. 'What are you doing over there?' he said irritably. The irritability would have been recognized by any half-baked psychologist as a displacement activity. 'You know I don't like anything going on behind my back. No soldier ever does.'

'Just looking,' said Helen, feeling suddenly rebellious. From now on there would be no need to play the subservient daughter ever again.

'Well, come where I can see you,' he ordered.

'They've got everything here, haven't they?' Helen said, looking round the walls, and not moving, 'except shrunken heads.'

'I dare say,' said her sister drily, 'they ought to have some of those, too.'

'One, anyway,' said Helen.

'So,' said Walter Bryant, affecting not to have heard this, 'I've arranged for Miss Ritchie – Margot – to come in this morning to have coffee with us so you can congratulate her and hear about our wedding plans.'

Agnes drew in her breath sharply but her father was already looking at his watch. Before she could speak he said, 'She'll be here any minute now . . .'

But meeting Miss Ritchie just at this minute was something his daughters could not bring themselves to do. They left immediately without farewell kisses.

*

Berebury Police Station was a relatively quiet place on Saturday mornings. Like birds of prey, evildoers tended not to rise too early in the day. Avian raptors need rising thermals of spiralling hot air in which to soar above their quarry – malefactors seek darkness and a tired waning of attention in their potential victims. Detective Inspector Sloan and Detective Constable Crosby were therefore sitting in an almost empty canteen. They were drinking tea and concentrating on a list.

'If you ask me,' said Crosby, 'they go to that Manor and forget to die.'

'Not this lot,' said Sloan, tapping the paper. 'These are the ones who went there and did die.'

Crosby sniffed. 'I dare say, sir, but you can't say that any of them were exactly knocked-off in their prime, can you?'

'We can't say that any of them were knocked-off at all,' retorted Sloan with some asperity. Jumping to conclusions was something a properly professional detective constable should have learned by now not to do. That way led to miscarriages of justice on a grand scale – and compensation on an even grander one. 'Not even Gertrude Powell.' He paused and said thoughtfully, making a mental note, 'Especially not her.'

'But . . .'

'These,' Sloan waved the paper at him, 'are just the names of all eight of the residents of the Manor who have died in the past three years, starting with a Lionel MacFarlane.'

'Knocking-on, all of 'em,' insisted the constable, 'even if they weren't knocked-off.'

'Their ages,' said Sloan grandly, 'have got nothing to do with it. A crime is a crime is a crime.'

This was Sloan's own private adaptation of Gertrude Stein's famous syllogism 'A rose is a rose is a rose.' He'd been very taken by this statement when he'd seen it plastered all over a catalogue from his favourite plant nursery. He'd given it quite a lot of thought while trying to make up his mind between buying a new *Rosa banksiae* or another Picasso rose bush.

Crosby's brow furrowed into a deep frown of incomprehension as he drained his mug.

'A victim is always a victim,' said Sloan. He didn't think Crosby would understand the connection with roses even if he explained it to him. The constable wasn't an inveterate rose grower and Sloan was. This was no accident. There weren't very many recreations open to a busy detective inspector liable to be called back to duty at the drop of a hat – or the raising of a weapon – but growing roses was one of them.

Crosby's brow cleared a little.

'And if any of these people on this list have died unnaturally then they are still victims,' said Sloan, raising a hand in salute to his friend and colleague Inspector Harpe of Traffic Division, who had just come into the canteen. Now, Harpe's hobby was keeping tropical fish. Fish didn't mind being left. Like roses, they waited.

'You wouldn't think it'd matter so much, all the same,' said the voice of youth sitting opposite him. 'All these people over at Almstone must have been going to die very soon anyway, if not sooner.'

'And,' carried on Sloan, undeterred by this tempting philosophical byway, 'whoever brought about their deaths . . .'

'If they did,' Crosby put in a caveat.

'If they did,' agreed Sloan, 'is still a murderer.'

Detective Constable Crosby plunged his face into his mug of tea and said slyly, 'Even if, sir, it was their own doctor?'

'Ay,' thought Sloan privately, 'there's the rub.' Shakespeare had put his finger on it, all right. The beneficent action, the best of intentions, the greatest good for the greatest number . . . a flood of half-remembered, half-thought-out justifications tumbled into mind, some of them relics of courtroom battles. The extent of what could be found to be said in mitigation by defence counsel always came as a surprise to him – and probably to the accused, too.

The trouble was that none of the arguments was conclusive – satisfactory, even. Not even his own personal belief that actions taken in malice ought not to succeed. And what about that tricky one – bad action taken with bad intent that had a good outcome? He didn't know. He was only a policeman.

Aloud he said, 'That, Crosby, is what the doctors call the defence of the double effect.'

'Really, sir?'

'The general idea is if the doctor is only setting out to kill the pain, then death is only a side effect.'

'More tea, sir?' Crosby interrupted this disquisition. 'Before we start chasing up that list.'

'What's that?' Sloan jerked back to the here and now. Some things were better left to the moralists. 'Oh, yes, thank you.'

He was not deceived. Crosby's way to the canteen counter – and his way back – would let Inspector Harpe become aware of his presence. Harpe was known throughout the Calleshire Force as Happy Harry on account of his never having been seen to smile. His contention that there never was anything in Traffic Division at which to smile was only likely to have been reinforced by Detective Constable Crosby's best efforts to join it.

Sloan turned back to the names of those who had died at the Manor.

They read like a roll-call of the Scottish army at the Battle of Flodden plus camp followers. The only name that meant anything to him was that of Maude Chalmers-Hyde; she whom Dr Browne had suspected of dying too soon. He must tell Crosby to get hold of copies of the death certificates of all the others – and the balance sheet of the Manor. The wisdom of always 'taking a look at the accounts' was something born of hard experience.

Many a showy outfit, Sloan had good reason to know, was without financial substance; many an unobtrusive enterprise was backed by big money. He'd have a look at the Manor's Trust Deed while he was about it. Grateful patients might have left them money and indigent ones been hastened on their way. The other side of the coin in more ways than one, you might say . . .

'Your tea, sir.' Crosby interrupted his thoughts by plonking the mug down on the table with a vigour that splattered drops of hot liquid – if nothing else, their canteen tea was always hot and wet – all over the list of those deceased.

'You're in luck, Crosby,' observed Sloan pleasantly.

'Sir?'

'I'm going to give you the time to do out this muster list again.' Inspector Harpe, Sloan was happy to see, had not allowed Crosby to catch his eye as he passed.

'Yes, sir.'

Sloan pushed the damp sheet of paper back to the constable. 'Anything else you can make of this lot?'

Superintendent Leeyes might not be in the police station but he had made his presence felt by leaving a wordy memo about the importance of immediately reporting to him the results of their morning's investigations.

'More women than men,' said Crosby at once.

'Women live longer. Even at the Manor – ' Sloan pulled himself up with a jerk. He mustn't jump to conclusions either.

Crosby shrugged his shoulders. 'Old soldiers must be getting pretty thin on the ground now anyway. Long time no war,' he said, submerging Korea, Malaya, Northern Ireland, the Falklands Campaign and the Gulf War without a second thought – to say nothing of those notoriously dangerous military exercises, peacetime manoeuvres.

'I think the Super will want a little more than . . .'

Crosby waved his hand airily. 'Don't worry, sir. He won't be in this morning.'

'No?'

'On duty on the domestic front,' said Crosby. 'His wife makes him take her to the supermarket Saturday mornings. He doesn't get to play golf Sundays otherwise. Didn't you know, sir?'

'No,' said Sloan, considerably entertained, 'and how, may I ask, do you?'

'It's my landlady,' said the constable. 'She sees them there. She says Mrs Leeyes is a real tartar.'

Detective Inspector Sloan could well believe it. He'd seen the Superintendent's wife himself – a short, thin, shrewish woman with a tongue like a whiplash. At the police station she was uncharitably credited with being the reason for her husband's irascibility. Sloan found it oddly comforting that his boss shouldn't be in charge at home. Now, that was one thing he, Christopher Dennis Sloan, didn't have to worry about ... Suddenly a vision of the rose catalogue came unbidden into his mind. The choice between *Rosa banksiae*, a very vigorous climber which could reach thirty feet, and the rose bush Picasso, a two-foot-high shrub, had eventually come down in favour of the smaller rose. Their suburban garden, his wife, Margaret, had pointed out with gentle persistence, wasn't really quite big enough for such vigorous climbers.

He stood up abruptly, scraping his chair on the floor. 'Come on, Crosby, let's go and see what this lot got up to in the war.'

The Regimental History of the Fearnshires was full of names familiar to the two policemen but attached to much junior ranks. The Judge figured as a mere Captain while Peter Markyate and Donald Tulloch had been Second Lieutenants. The account of the Tinchel written in the dry words of the professional military historian was in its way even more stirring than any amount of emotional purple prose would have been.

At Wadi el Gebra, A Company of the 3rd Battalion of the Fearnshires, under the command of Major Lionel MacFarlane, had held out against heavy odds. Captain Calum Gillespie had led a secondary decoy action ...

'That's the Judge,' remarked Sloan.

'Crafty, even then,' opined Crosby.

... while Lieutenant Walter Bryant, although

severely wounded, had acted with extreme gallantry in defending the Company's position.

'Got it in the legs,' said Crosby, who had been known to complain about the rigours of the beat.

Second Lieutenant Peter Markyate had led the break-out of the encirclement.

'You wouldn't have thought he had it in him, would you?' said Crosby.

'That was then,' said Sloan.

And, ran the history, Second Lieutenant Hector Carruthers . . .

'He must have been the husband of the woman who arrived the day before yesterday,' said Sloan, reminding himself to have a word with her. She had obviously known the Brigadier, at least of old.

. . . had distinguished himself in action. Other casualties had included Captain Roderick Forbes, wounded . . .

'Where, I wonder,' murmured Sloan, shutting the book, 'was our Hamish MacIver at the time or Mrs McBeath's husband?'

'Search me,' said Detective Constable Crosby helpfully.

Chapter Thirteen

When they, pale captives, creep to death

Lionel Powell came away from the telephone at his home in suburban Luston shouting, 'Julia! Julia! Where are you?'

Julia winced. Noise didn't help her headache. 'Here,' she called unsteadily.

He made towards the direction whence the sound had come and found his wife sitting at the kitchen table nursing a cup of black coffee in both hands, her ample figure crammed untidily into a jumper and skirt.

'What's wrong?' she asked. She looked as if she had slept in her clothes, although he knew she hadn't.

Lionel Powell tightened his lips. 'I really don't know what's going on over at the Manor.'

'What does it matter?' she asked. 'After all, your mother's gone now.'

'Of course it matters, my dear.' Not for the first time, he experienced an involuntary pang of sympathy as he looked at his wife. She was a woman who somehow contrived to look raddled without having enjoyed – except now and then – the excesses of life.

'I don't see why.'

'But,' he said aggrievedly, 'I couldn't get any sense out of them at all. They sounded completely at sixes and sevens . . .'

'I expect they're still worrying about that silly letter of your mother's.'

'And I only rang to say we were on our way over to collect that amulet thing of Mother's and hand it over to Captain Markyate—'

He was interrupted by his wife. 'I said you should never have given it to the Manor.'

Actually Julia had said that she thought the library at the Manor was the best place for anything so peculiar, but Lionel knew better than to remind her of this. Julia was always a great one for being wise after the event. 'You never liked it,' he pointed out, 'and I must say neither did I.'

'I still don't like it,' she said.

'How was I to know that Mother had particularly wanted it given to Markyate?' he demanded of the world at large.

'Trust your mother,' said Julia obscurely.

'I just didn't think it was somehow quite right to open her Letter of Intent until after the funeral, that's all.'

'Not decent,' agreed Julia, spoiling the effect by saying, 'What's a Letter of Intent?'

'A statement you leave for your executors with your will which isn't actually part of it.' Lionel was always at his best stating – and restating – unvarnished fact.

Julia pushed some coffee in his direction. She frowned. 'What's the point of that?'

'It's how you tell them what you want doing with items too small to be mentioned individually in the will itself. Keepsakes and so forth.'

Julia suddenly sat up straight. 'Such as jewellery?'

'No. Such as that wretched amulet,' said Lionel sourly, 'which I am told the police have taken away for further examination. Not that it matters too much in law what happens to it.'

'Oh?'

'It's not the same as if it was in the will,' explained her husband.

'In what way?'

'Then we'd have had to do everything she had wanted.'

This was clearly a new concept to Julia. 'You really mean the executors don't have to do everything the Letter of Intent says?'

'Yes. They don't. Or more precisely,' Lionel Powell enjoyed being precise, 'the executors of the will cannot be challenged in law for not disposing of items in the Letter of Intent exactly as requested.'

Julia suddenly looked quite shrewish. 'That

means that they can be asked about the things in the will proper? That's if they don't do the right thing by the dead person?'

'Oh, yes.'

'But who would do that?'

'I suppose theoretically anyone could,' he said, 'but in the ordinary way it would be the heirs who did the challenging if they weren't happy with the way things had been handled.'

Julia Powell replaced her coffee cup on the table. 'Those heirs of the body female in the will?'

'In this instance, yes.' As he drained his coffee he was assailed by another unhappy thought. 'Or by anyone who thought they should have been an heir and who wasn't.'

'Lionel,' Julia said in a small voice, 'had you thought . . .'

'Yes,' he said harshly. 'I've thought about it a lot.'

'She would have been capable of bigamy,' said Julia. 'Enjoyed it, I expect.'

'My mother would have been capable of anything,' he said feelingly. 'Anything at all.'

Julia Powell was not a notably intelligent woman but she was right up there with her husband when she said, 'It would explain her leaving everything to her heirs of the body female, wouldn't it?'

'That would cut out any previous husband still living from whom she had not been divorced before she went through a ceremony of marriage with my father,' said the only child of that latter union with accuracy, all feeling tightly suppressed.

'That's what I thought,' said his helpmeet.

The last Will and Testament of Gertude Eleanor Murton Powell was something which Detective Inspector Sloan was also studying with care and attention.

He and Detective Constable Crosby were both doing this with the assistance of young Mr Simon Puckle of Messrs Puckle, Puckle and Nunnery, Solicitors and Notaries Public, of Berebury. Young Simon Puckle wasn't actually young but so called to distinguish him from one of his uncles. They had met at the firm's offices in the town at Sloan's request.

'It's a very old will,' said the solicitor disapprovingly. 'Actually it's one drawn up by my late grandfather . . . nothing wrong with it, of course.'

'Of course,' said Sloan, who remembered Simon's grandfather well. Old Mr Puckle had been a solicitor of the old school, capable of striking a good deal more terror into any client caught in wrongdoing than the police would ever have dared to do.

'We do like clients to update their wills more often than this,' frowned the solicitor.

'Quite so,' said Sloan. He himself had been brought up on the principle that a man's financial affairs should always be conducted as if he were going to live for ever and his family ones as if he were going to die tomorrow.

'Wills,' said the solicitor severely, 'should be revised at least every three years.'

'I'm sure,' said Sloan, who actually wasn't at all sure if this advice was for the benefit of client or lawyer.

'Because that's at least three new Finance Acts,' said Simon Puckle.

'Is it still valid though?' asked Sloan pertinently.

'Oh, yes, Inspector. It's been perfectly properly drawn up and signed and attested.' He held it between his fingers. 'The only unusual thing about it is that we – the firm, that is – agreed to be joint executors and trustees with a man who had barely come of age at the time, but I understand from my grandfather's notes that Mrs Powell was quite adamant about her son being appointed in spite of his extreme youth when the will was drawn up.'

'And I gather, Mr Puckle, that the late Mrs Powell had a mind of her own.' The legal profession and the police were obviously both of the opinion that it was a good thing that 'Youth's a stuff will not endure.'

'There is one advantage,' said Simon Puckle cannily, 'of it's being such an old will . . .'

'Tell me.'

'It is unlikely that there can be any valid suggestion that the testatrix was not mentally competent to make a will at the time she did.'

Sloan inclined his head. 'That is useful to know.'

At least, then, the deceased had been in full possession of her faculties when she had put her name to the document and not 'Over the hills and far away.' What he would dearly liked to have been quite sure about was whether the same could be said for when Gertie Powell had written her last letter to her son.

'It can get a bit tricky as time goes by,' admitted the solicitor. 'Especially when the testatrix has been a patient in a nursing home for months – years, perhaps.'

'I can see that it might,' agreed Sloan.

'Moreover,' complained the lawyer, 'we find that these days some registered medical practitioners are not as willing as they once were to agree to be witnesses to wills.'

'Really?' Detective Inspector Sloan tried to sound suitably concerned at the man's discovery that dog did indeed eat dog – or rather at the failure of one professional to get something out of another professional for nothing. Puckle should have known this by now. 'Now,' he said, 'if you would outline the contents of the will for us . . .'

'The late Gertrude Powell left everything of which she died possessed, save for some minor dispositions of a personal and sentimental nature, equally to all her heirs of the body female.'

'And that means?'

'To all the children to whom she had given birth,' explained Simon Puckle succinctly. 'And *per stirpes*

– should they have predeceased their mother and had children, to those children.'

'So Lionel Powell might have to share . . .'

'If we should find there are or have been other children with living issue of other marriages.'

'I see.'

'So naturally after her death we started to make enquiries,' said Simon Puckle sedately.

'And?'

'As far as we have been able to establish through the usual channels, Mrs Powell's first marriage – that was to the late Second Lieutenant Donald Tulloch of the Fearnshires – was childless.' He coughed. 'We certainly have no evidence to the contrary.'

'I see.' Detective Inspector Sloan made a note.

Simon Puckle hesitated. 'The problems arise after that.'

'What problems?' asked Sloan. The only interest the police had was in whether any problems might have been solved – not created – by the death of an old lady. An old lady who had asserted that she had been murdered.

'We have reason to think she entered into another marriage – quite possibly in 1942 or 1943 while she was still in Egypt . . . we know she stayed on in Alexandria after her first husband was killed in action – and though there is no evidence of this in our records, Lionel Powell has always believed it to be so.'

Detective Inspector Sloan glanced down at his

notebook. 'Not the man by whom she had Lionel Powell, then?'

Puckle shook his head. 'No. That marriage – it is thought, her third – was later still.' He coughed and said drily, 'She gave the name of Smith when she married Hubert Powell, which has not proved particularly helpful when it has come to tracing her second marriage.' He hesitated. 'Both her son and ourselves as executors were hoping to find all the relevant details among her papers after her death and thus obviate a long search but . . .'

Detective Constable Crosby uncoiled his length from the leather chair opposite the solicitor and said laconically, 'But someone beat you all to it, didn't they? They took her letters before Lionel got there.'

Chapter Fourteen

The garlands wither on your brow

'The fact that the deceased's letters went missing just as soon as she died must mean,' said Sloan, speaking as much to himself as to Detective Constable Crosby, 'that – like it or not – at least some of the answers to all this carry-on must lie at the Manor.'

Superintendent Leeyes wouldn't like it, that was for sure. Crosby on the other hand did not even sound particularly interested when he said, 'An inside job.'

'It also lends weight to the probability of the deceased's last letter to her son being genuine,' said Sloan, thankful that at long last he had been able to achieve a few minutes back at his own desk in Berebury Police Station.

'It is for real, sir,' said Crosby, passing him a message sheet. 'This has just come in. That handwriting woman . . .'

'Graphologist is what she likes to be called,' murmured Sloan.

' . . . graphologist, then, who we sent that copy over to yesterday with something else she'd written is prepared to swear to the letter being in the old lady's handwriting.'

Detective Inspector Sloan said he was glad to have something amounting to a fact in the case because as far as he knew they hadn't got very many to date.

'There's the letters going missing from the deceased's bedroom, sir,' said Crosby. 'Surely that's evidence?'

'A factor – no more.'

'And there being no fingerprints on that ornament thing . . .'

'I understand,' said Sloan austerely, 'that the technical term is artefact.'

'It's not natural,' insisted Crosby, 'not to have fingerprints on something that old.'

'True. But all it might mean is that somebody just cleaned them off for hygiene's sake.'

'Then,' said Crosby, undeterred in his theoretical endeavours, 'there's that funny old boy upstairs who threw a wobbly over someone doing up his ancient coat. That's odd enough, isn't it? Sounds as if a tramp would have turned it down. Then there's the deceased . . .'

'I suppose,' said Detective Inspector Sloan fairly, 'an allegation of murder is in itself evidence of something – if only of a mind deranged.'

'We do have something else, sir,' said the detective constable, warming to his theme.

'We do?'

'Yes, sir. There's those two doctors disagreeing with each other.'

'Differing,' Sloan corrected him. 'That's all doctors do. They just agree to differ.'

Crosby looked quite blank. 'Isn't that the same as disagreeing?'

'Not when it's doctors,' said Sloan ironically. 'Then it's called professional courtesy.'

'Well, whatever,' said Crosby, 'one doctor wouldn't certify that Maude Chalmers-Hyde had died naturally and the other doctor said she had.'

'That's true.' Sloan nodded. Crosby had remembered something, then, from the mortuary.

'Then next time round the first doctor goes and says Gertrude Powell died from natural causes . . .'

'And so does the second doctor,' Sloan reminded him.

'But the deceased says someone was going to kill her . . .'

' . . . had killed her,' Sloan corrected him, his mind going on to something else. 'Does,' he wondered aloud, 'the fact that her son handed on to us that letter to him from her lend weight to the probability of its being genuine or are we supposed to think he's a good boy and therefore not guilty of any malfeasance? That's been done before . . .'

'Couldn't say, I'm sure, sir,' responded the detective constable blithely. 'Proper old fusspot, our little Lionel, isn't he?'

'Attention to detail,' said Sloan, 'is what makes a successful murderer – and a good police officer, Crosby, too. Remember that.'

'Yes, sir.' He cogitated for a moment and then said, 'If Lionel Powell had hung on to that letter and not said a dicky bird to anyone no one would have been any the wiser, would they?'

Detective Inspector Sloan turned over a new page in his notebook. 'In theory, no. But that, Crosby, presupposes that no one apart from the writer of the letter and its recipient were aware of its contents.'

'Yes, sir.'

'We know that Hazel Finch knew of its existence because she told us so.'

'We know now.'

'It would have been difficult for Lionel Powell to have denied receiving it and there was always the risk that we might have asked to be shown it.'

A mulish look came over Crosby's features. 'Not if he hadn't said anything,' he muttered obstinately. 'Then we'd never have known to start looking for there being something wrong.'

'True,' said Sloan equably, not displeased with Crosby's line of reasoning. The constable always engaged gear before opening the throttle in a car but he didn't always engage the mind before opening the mouth. 'But there's another possibility . . .'

'Sir?'

'We might be being meant to catch some of his chickens for him as they come home to roost,' said Sloan.

'Us? Catspaws?' The constable considered the idea. It was clearly a new one to him.

'That's been done before, too,' said Sloan. 'But not often. Talking of which, Crosby, we had better get started on looking for this elusive second husband of hers.'

'Yes, sir.' The constable paused and then asked, 'How?'

'Ask the Registrar General's Office to forget about its being their weekend and please to do a search for the record of a marriage probably in Egypt between the two dates we know about . . . and quickly.'

Crosby's pencil hovered above his notebook. 'Which two dates, sir?'

Sloan sighed. 'The death of Donald Tulloch and the deceased's marriage to Hubert Powell.'

'When she called herself Smith?'

'It's still the commonest surname in Scotland,' Sloan assured him. 'Now, how did you get on with the Pragmatic Sanction?'

The detective constable scowled. 'Badly.' He read aloud from his notebook. 'The first were decrees issued by Kings of France restricting the rights of the Pope and making some of them subject to the jurisdiction of the king.'

'I can't see myself exactly what that could have to do with the Manor at Almstone.' He frowned. 'But go on.'

'And the next one was signed in 1713 by Emperor Charles VI.' He consulted his notes. 'It was a sort of will leaving everything to his eldest son first, failing whom his eldest daughter, and then to his deceased brother's daughters.'

'Sounds to me,' said Sloan, who'd attended the Family Division of the Courts in his day, 'as if he'd wanted to cut someone out.' He frowned. 'That might be very relevant indeed to events at the Manor.'

'The history book,' Crosby ploughed on, 'said he'd wanted to hand down an undivided heritage.'

'So might that,' said Sloan. It had been, after all, the late Gertrude Powell who had used the term.

'But it didn't work.'

'No?'

Crosby went back to his notebook. 'Led to the War of the Austrian Succession. Then . . .'

'There were more?'

'Sort of. King Ferdinand of Spain revoked the Salic Law of Succession in 1830.'

The Salic Law was something from Sloan's own history lessons that had stuck. Or very nearly. Under Salic law, wives, he remembered, could not inherit from their husbands.

Crosby had encountered another part of it. 'That, sir, was permitting an unborn child to succeed even if female.'

'Any minute now, Crosby, you'll be making out a case for feminism.'

'Pardon, sir?'

'Nothing. Go on.'

'Actually Charles IV had already decided on all this in 1789 when he restored the Act abr– abrogated in 1713.'

'It means annul,' said Sloan, wondering if there might be a connection there, too, with recent events at the Manor at Almstone.

'But,' went on Crosby, 'Charles hadn't told anyone he'd done it.'

It had been another King Charles and a quite different secret treaty that Sloan had been taught about at school. That was Charles II of England and the secret treaty and the camouflage treaty he had signed at Dover in 1670. A secret arrangement of some sort might have quite a lot to do with the deceased at Almstone. And so might camouflage. But which was secret and which was camouflage was something else.

'That,' finished Crosby conscientiously, 'led to the Wars of the Supporters of Don Carlos.'

'What I want to know, Crosby,' said Sloan, slapping his notebook shut, 'is exactly where that leaves us at the Manor.'

But answer came there none.

*

Ned Carruthers arrived at the Manor at half-past eleven and swept into his mother's room armed with a large bunch of flowers.

'Stella sends her love,' he lied, presenting Maisie with a considerable bouquet of scent and colour.

'How kind,' said Maisie ambiguously.

Ned pulled a chair up beside his mother's bed, responded to her perfunctory enquiries about her daughter-in-law with more lies, and then asked her how she had been getting on.

'The food's not what I'm used to,' she said. That was technically true – the tea and toast on which she had been subsisting before her accident didn't compare with Lisa Haines' best efforts. 'And the bed's too hard.'

He bent forward to examine it. 'I'm sure something can be done about that.'

'My hip still hurts, too,' she said, pulling the bedclothes tightly around her lest he offer to inspect that as well.

'I'm sorry,' he said, forbearing to make any comment on her newly waved hair and remarkably alert mien. 'Are they giving you anything for it?'

'Tablets,' she said scornfully. 'Tablets and more tablets.'

'You may feel better when you've settled down.' Ned always advised his landscaping clients that plants and soil needed time to settle.

'It's all very well for you,' she responded tartly.

'You haven't been condemned to live here for the rest of your life like I have.'

Her son wriggled uneasily in his chair. 'You shouldn't say that, Mummy. It isn't a prison sentence.'

'Isn't it?' she shot back.

'No, Mummy, it certainly is not.'

'No?' She pursed her lips and appeared to consider the matter. 'No, perhaps not. Perhaps it's more of a death sentence.'

'Of course it isn't a death sentence. You shouldn't talk like that.'

'For the crime of being old.'

'Nonsense. It's a big change coming to a place like this. That's all. You must expect it to take time to get used to.' Ned's clients were always told that they – like the plants – would need to become accustomed to the changes he had wrought on their land.

'Moreover,' she said, ignoring his platitudes with practised ease, 'it's no joke giving up one's independence.'

'You've still got an independent mind, Mummy. They can't take that away from you.'

Maisie Carruthers gave a satisfied nod. 'That's true. They can't stop me thinking what I want to think.'

'I should hope not. Have you,' he ventured carefully, 'happened to come across any old friends here yet?'

A guarded look came over her face. 'Not friends

exactly. More what I'd call people I've known from way back.'

'What about Peter Markyate?'

'He hasn't changed. Once a bumbler, always a bumbler.'

'I don't think I'd recognize him now if I saw him,' said Ned Carruthers, drifting as usual towards the window, the better to see the Manor's grounds. 'I'm wondering if there's an old ha-ha out there.'

'Plenty of those in here,' said his mother ungraciously. 'It's what the men actually say when they've forgotten what it was they were going to say in the first place. Old fools.'

But Ned wasn't listening. 'Do you know, Mummy, I think the Manor could have been built on an ancient moated site. Now, that would be really interesting . . .'

'Would it?' she said drily.

He turned his head in another direction. 'I say, I think something must be happening outside here.'

'What?' She struggled up from her pillows. 'Where?'

'In the garden over to the left.'

'That's what they call the hither green,' said Maisie. 'I don't know why.'

'Then,' said Ned abstractedly, his attention engaged by what he was looking at, 'ten to one there'll be a thither one beyond.'

'Never mind that. Tell me what's going on.'

'Half the staff are out there rushing about . . .'

The tight bedclothes on his mother's bed were

cast aside with unexpected energy as she reached for her stick and hirpled vigorously across the bedroom floor, all pretence of immobility gone.

'Here, let me see,' she said, elbowing Ned out of the way.

'And look,' Ned pointed, 'there's a police car turning into the drive.'

'What are all those people doing in the bushes?'

'If you ask me,' said Ned, 'they're looking for someone.'

'But who?' asked his mother urgently. 'That's what matters. Don't you realize that?'

It wasn't Judge Gillespie. Hazel Finch had spent half the morning attending to him. It hadn't been easy work, either.

'You're all to pieces today, Judge,' she complained. 'I don't know why you're so shaky, I'm sure.'

The Judge's tremor, always present, was now very pronounced indeed.

'You'd better let me shave you,' said Hazel. 'Next thing we know you'll be cutting your throat.'

'Or having it cut for me,' he piped. His voice was now the childish treble of Shakespeare's seventh age of man.

'You shouldn't talk like that,' Hazel reproved him, shocked. 'Who'd ever want to do such a thing?'

The old man didn't answer her. Instead he said, 'Hazel, will you do something for me?'

'Of course I will, Judge.' She paused. 'As long as it isn't posting letters after you've gone. Mite of trouble that seems to have caused.'

'Nothing like that, m'dear, I promise you.' Through ancient teeth, he achieved the parody of a grimace. 'No, all I want you to do when you go home today is to take my torch down to Mr Mason's in the village. It needs new batteries and he'll put them in for me. Tell him to keep the torch until I call for it – I'll soon be out and about again. I'm much better already.'

'I could bring you the batteries myself, Monday,' offered Hazel, 'if you like.'

Judge Gillespie bestowed on her the kindly smile that had misled many a barrister in his time. 'That's very thoughtful of you, m'dear, but if there's one thing that a long life has taught me it's that women and electricity don't mix.' He essayed a wheezy chuckle. 'My late wife was always asking where it went when you took the plug out.'

'Fancy that,' said Hazel, who wasn't at all sure either where electricity went when you weren't using it. 'I expect Mrs Gillespie was good at other things.' One of the tenets of good care that all the staff of the Manor had had instilled in them by the well-trained and conscientious Muriel Peden was the importance of encouraging the residents to talk about their deceased spouses when the opportunity arose. 'Did she do the flowers?' The care assistant's idea of the leisured woman was one who always had time to spend doing the flowers.

'What? Oh, yes . . .' he said vaguely, submitting to a warm towel and a shaving brush. 'She always did them very well.'

'Now keep still,' adjured Hazel. 'After all that I don't want to be the one who cuts you.'

Judge Gillespie suddenly became very meek.

Hazel was still struggling to get him dressed when she was sent for to join a search party.

Chapter Fifteen

Then boast no more your mighty deeds

The message from the Manor had reached Sloan and Crosby at the police station. It had come from Matron herself by telephone.

She had sounded concerned but not over-anxious – one professional conveying information to another professional in as neutral a way as possible. And in diminutives when she could.

'I wouldn't have bothered you at this stage in the ordinary way,' Muriel Peden began apologetically, 'but . . .' The end of the sentence dangled, unspoken, in the air.

'Quite so.' Detective Inspector Sloan's agreement was tacit. Whatever it was that was going on at the Manor was not ordinary, he was already convinced about that. 'Tell me.'

'It's Mrs McBeath.'

'What about her?'

'She isn't in her room.'

'Should she be there in the middle of the

morning?' Policemen could play at this game of being laid-back as well as nurses.

'Not necessarily, but . . .'

'But?'

'But more importantly,' Muriel Peden audibly drew in her breath, 'I understand she didn't come down to breakfast this morning.'

'When do you check the rooms?'

He got an oblique answer from the Matron. 'Most of our residents like a cup of tea first thing.'

'First thing?' queried Sloan sharply. That timing would be too imprecise for Superintendent Leeyes for a start.

'Early,' she said defensively. 'Old people don't sleep well, that is unless—'

'Unless?' he interrupted her again. The word 'early' wasn't exactly pinpointing the time either.

'Unless they're on sleeping tablets.'

'Ah! Who doles out their tablets?' He checked himself. He should have asked who administered them but 'doling out' seemed to be the order of the day in the medicated world of today.

'We do. The nursing staff, that is. But Mrs McBeath . . .'

Sloan made a mental note. That was definitely something he should have thought through before: that all the medicines at the Manor would be kept together in one place. Under lock and key, no doubt, but every policeman learned early that love wasn't the only thing that laughed at locksmiths. Murderers did, too.

'But Mrs McBeath . . .'

'But Mrs McBeath doesn't take them.'

'She sleeps well?'

'She sleeps badly,' explained Muriel Peden awkwardly, 'but she won't take any medication for it. Got quite upset when it was suggested.'

Sloan made another mental note. 'So when do you check the room?' he asked again.

'We don't.'

Sloan ground his teeth. That was something else the Superintendent would not like.

'At least,' hurried on the Matron, 'not Mrs McBeath's room. Some, but not hers. She likes to be left undisturbed, so if she's had a bad night, she may sleep on.'

'So?'

'So when she didn't appear by coffee-time one of the girls went up to check that she was all right.'

'And she wasn't there?' Sloan motioned to Detective Constable Crosby to start to get ready for the road.

'Her room was empty.' The Matron swallowed. 'And so we don't know whether she's all right or not.'

'Bed slept in?' If parameters of time could not be got one way, then they would have to be got another – Superintendent Leeyes would pretty soon be playing the blame game if not.

'Oh, yes, but I'm afraid it's not as simple as that.'

Detective Inspector Sloan had already reached the conclusion that nothing at the Manor was simple any more than it was ordinary. 'In what way?'

'Since we've started looking for her several residents have told us they'd seen her pacing up and down in the grounds all morning looking distinctly agitated.'

'But you can't find her there?' Sloan was on his feet now.

'Not anywhere,' said Muriel Peden tightly.

'Well?' demanded Mrs Carruthers, deeply regretting her earlier decision to stay in bed that morning. She had straight away despatched her son downstairs to find out what had been going on in the garden and Ned had now come back to her room. 'Don't just stand there,' she said as he stayed silent.

'No, Mummy.'

'Then tell me who it is they are all looking for out there.'

'Someone called Mrs McBeath,' Ned said unwillingly. He had positioned himself just inside the bedroom, his back to the door.

'Mrs McBeath?' His mother sat straight up in her bed. 'Little Morag McBeath?'

'You may not know her,' murmured Ned hopefully.

'Of course I know her.'

'She's gone missing.'

'I don't believe it.'

'I expect she wandered off alone.'

Maisie glared at him. 'Rubbish!'

'Probably getting a bit old and all that,' he said awkwardly.

'She had all her wits yesterday. Nobody could have called her doited then,' she sniffed, 'which is more than you can say for some folk around here.'

Ned stiffened himself against the back of the door. 'I'm afraid they can't find her anywhere.'

'Afraid?' Maisie Carruthers turned her head away and looked towards the window, an unfathomable expression on her face. 'What do you mean?'

'That they're very worried that something might have happened to her.'

'Are you sure?'

He said, 'It's the police who are worried.'

Mrs Carruthers let her head sink gently downwards on to her chest. Ned couldn't see his mother's face at all now.

'They've just arrived from Berebury,' he ventured, wondering if Mrs McBeath might have collapsed in the garden. Dying in a garden when his time came was all he ever asked for himself, although he was enough of a professional to know that a garden was as much of a hell's half-acre as anywhere else. 'It's a good place to go, a garden, if you have to,' he went on lightly.

'Alone?' she said drily. 'And afraid?'

'No, perhaps it's not good to go alone,' he

conceded, wondering if this was what she had really meant. 'But,' he produced his favourite quotation, always very popular with lady garden-lovers of a certain age, ' "A garden is a lovesome thing. God wot!" ' He didn't believe it himself, of course. Plant, insect, rodent and bird carried on their struggles for survival in a garden just as they – and everything else – did everywhere else in the world.

Man, too, sometimes. And woman.

'How long has she been missing?' his mother asked presently.

'Since she was seen in the garden this morning.'

'Ah . . .' Maisie's expression was quite inscrutable. 'It's like that, is it?'

'We've all got to stay in our rooms until they've interviewed everyone.' Ned Carruthers was something of a garden historian as well as a landscape designer but this was not the moment for his celebrated little lecture on the wild man of the garden. The hermit had been in his grotto there to remind the visitor that evil – in the shape of a wild man – lurked at the bottom of the garden, that there was always danger there.

'Even us?'

Ned nodded. 'Even us. We've got to stay here until they come.' The lineal descendant of the hermit in his grotto was the fear of seeing something nasty in the woodshed – and quite probably the Mr McGregor who had so frightened Peter Rabbit . . .

'I can't tell them anything.'

'Of course you can't,' he said warmly. 'You've only just got here. You mustn't worry about it. It's nothing to do with you.'

A frown crossed his mother's forehead. 'But I don't understand why . . .'

'Why what?' He was worried now, she looked suddenly so old and defenceless. Besides, there was ever present the lurking fear that his mother might discharge herself from the Manor – and he knew exactly what his wife, Stella, would say about that, because she had already told him in no uncertain terms.

Several times.

Maisie said, 'But why Morag McBeath?'

'I don't understand, Mummy.' He wondered now if it was his mother who was confused. 'What do you mean?'

'I can't understand why it should have been Morag McBeath who's gone missing,' she repeated.

'We don't know why, either,' he said soothingly. 'But I'm sure they'll tell us all in good time. When she's turned up again.'

She wasn't listening. 'Because, you see, Charlie McBeath was on the Staff the whole time.'

'No,' he retorted, 'I don't see. What has Charlie McBeath got to do with it?'

'Nothing. That's the point.'

'He was her husband, I take it?'

'Yes.'

'So?'

161

'Charlie McBeath never left Alexandria.'

'What on earth are you talking about, Mummy?'

'Never you mind.' Maisie Carruthers clamped her edentulous jaws tightly together.

Try as he might, her son couldn't get her to say another word.

As the police car turned into the drive of the Manor at Almstone once again Detective Inspector Sloan saw fit to remark to Detective Constable Crosby, who was at the wheel at the time, that the gravel chippings there had not been laid down for the express purpose of his skidding to a dramatic halt thereon.

'Of course not, sir.' Crosby sounded injured. He pulled the police car round to the front door as if it had been the carriage and pair that the drive had been designed for and executed a gentle stop worthy of any professional chauffeur.

Mrs Muriel Peden was standing at the front door at the top of the short flight of steps and between two polished granite curling stones. She gave a negative shake of her head as they got out of the car. 'Not a sign of Mrs McBeath anywhere, I'm afraid, Inspector.'

Sloan cast his eyes round the grounds. The gardens stretched as far as he could see, giving way in a structured artistic recession of shades of green to great parkland trees. He said, 'We're going to need more than a good eye for country to know where to begin here, Matron.'

'The Brigadier's insisted on organizing a search party already,' Muriel Peden sighed, opening her hands wide in a gesture of helplessness. 'I couldn't stop him, Inspector. He's sent poor Captain Markyate to work his way towards the front gates and he's taken the back of the house and the car park himself.'

Sloan nodded. Presumably the Brigadier had a soldier's eye for country. It would, Sloan decided, be different from the police one.

'And Miss Bentley's checking the kitchen gardens, although what Mrs McBeath would be doing there and how Miss Bentley'll manage with her stick I don't know.'

'Crosby can go and see,' suggested Sloan, 'can't you, Crosby?'

'Yes, sir,' he said, obediently peeling off in the direction of the kitchen.

'It's all very well for you, Constable,' said Lisa Haines, encountering Crosby on his way to the kitchen door, 'but, missing persons or not, people have got to eat.'

The King might be in this counting house counting out his money and the Queen in the parlour eating bread and honey but – *mutatis mutandis* – any upset still found the cook in the kitchen making apple crumble in quantity.

'It's a missing person all right,' said Crosby, adding importantly, 'We're very worried about her.'

'It's chicken pie . . .'

'Leftovers from yesterday,' divined the constable.

'I'll have you know, young man,' said Lisa Haines grandly, 'that it's called "knock-on cookery".'

'Whatever it's called,' retorted Crosby, 'everyone who's indoors has got to go to their rooms and stay there until we say so.'

'That's as may be,' said the cook with spirit, 'but I've got my ovens to see to. I'm not leaving them to go and twiddle my thumbs in some sitting room, not with those pies in them.'

'I've come to guard the kitchen door, too,' said the constable. 'No one's to go out of here. Not now we're in charge.'

Lisa Haines jerked her shoulder towards the window and said slyly, 'What about coming in? All right to do that, is it?'

Detective Constable Crosby peered out at a majestic figure making her stately way through the kitchen garden. 'Who's that?'

A small smile hovered round the corners of the cook's lips. 'That's our Miss Bentley making sure nothing nasty's been going on under the gooseberry bushes. You'll enjoy her.'

Miss Bentley, leaning heavily on a stout walking stick, continued her progress, brown Oxford shoes and all, towards the kitchen door.

'Really,' she exclaimed, stumping into the kitchen

and plonking herself down on the nearest chair, 'this place is getting worse than Nightmare Abbey. Whatever next?'

A grammatical purist might have wondered why Miss Bentley hadn't said 'whoever' rather than 'whatever' but the former headteacher belonged to the Superintendent Leeyes school of taking bad news as a personal affront rather than as an occasion for sympathy for the victim.

'We'll be taking statements from everyone about when they last saw Mrs McBeath,' said Detective Constable Crosby, taking her question about 'whatever next' literally.

'It's when we next see her that matters,' snorted Miss Bentley, 'if we do. Silly woman.' Like the Superntendent, she too went in for victim-blaming. 'And how she is when we do find her . . . she could be anywhere in this rabbit warren of a place.'

'Standard procedure,' riposted the constable, speaking the language of officialdom well on this – but not every – occasion.

Miss Bentley, who might have been expected to have been on the side of the angels in the matters of both procedure and officialdom, made an indeterminate sound of dissent. 'That won't be the way to get at where she is, Constable.'

'In the Force, madam,' declared Crosby sonorously, 'we find truth will out. Even,' he added naively, 'if it does take its time about it sometimes.'

'Ah, yes.' Miss Bentley suddenly beamed her

agreement with this sentiment. One of her standard end-of-term addresses to the girls who were leaving had taken as its text the aphorism 'The truth may be blamed but it can never be shamed.' 'But not that way.'

'Tell me, what will be the way, then?' asked Crosby.

Miss Bentley didn't answer the question but gave it as her considered opinion that while she could think of no reason at all for Mrs McBeath to have come to any harm, she could think of one very good one for Miss Margot Ritchie meeting trouble instead.

Detective Constable Crosby sat down opposite her. 'You can?' he said encouragingly.

'I can.' Miss Bentley needed no encouraging. She had spent a lifetime pronouncing her strong views and having them treated with attention and respect. One of the many, many disappointments of retirement and old age had been that there were precious few people around now to listen to them.

Detective Constable Crosby leaned forward and made it very clear that he belonged to this small minority. 'Tell me,' he said with patent interest.

Miss Bentley was only too willing to expound her theories. These revolved round the subject of Walter Bryant and his expected remarriage. She asked, 'Well, wouldn't you prefer to live in a detached bungalow with a devoted wife and access to a motor vehicle instead of being permanently incarcerated in this benighted place?'

'Yes,' said Crosby simply.

'To say nothing of home comforts.' In the interests of her own future comfort Miss Bentley, no fool, decided against mentioning the delights of home cooking in the presence of Lisa Haines.

'Very important,' agreed Crosby, who was too young even to envisage old age let alone its attendant shortcomings.

'Take it from me,' she said darkly, 'those daughters of his will do anything they can to prevent the marriage.' With a visible effort Miss Bentley struggled to her feet and sailed out of the kitchen in the direction of the downstairs cloakroom.

He had barely had time to put his notebook away before she was back again, stickless and more than a little breathless.

'It's the Judge's coat,' she said dramatically. 'It's been slashed to absolute ribbons!'

Chapter Sixteen

Upon Death's purple altar now

'My old coat, you say? Really?' Two guileless blue eyes belonging to Judge Gillespie momentarily met those of Detective Inspector Sloan and then looked away. 'How very strange.'

What was stranger still in Sloan's view was that the Judge appeared to have lost a great deal of his tremulousness. Aged totterton he might still be, but his hands were much steadier than they had been the day before and his voice noticeably firmer.

'It was a very old coat,' the Judge added mildly. 'And like me, Inspector, it's been around for a long, long time.'

'It is now a very damaged one,' said Sloan.

While Sloan bearded the Judge in his own room, Detective Constable Crosby had been sent to summon police reinforcements from Berebury.

'It was practically worn out anyway,' said the Judge deprecatingly. 'It's no great loss.'

'Which makes the attack on it even more curious,' said Sloan firmly. He had been particularly anxious to be the very first person to talk to the nonagenarian about an ancient coat – and a missing elderly lady.

'It does indeed, Inspector.' The Judge's expression was quite fathomless.

'And we should like to know why.'

'Yes, of course, Inspector. I quite understand that.'

'What I don't understand, sir,' countered Sloan in a voice pregnant with meaning, 'is quite why someone should take it into their heads to cut an old coat to pieces.'

'Nor I,' said the Judge blandly.

'Your old coat . . .'

'My very old coat . . .'

'Practically shredded, you might say . . .'

'Shredded, eh?' Gillespie sounded positively spry now. 'How very curious.'

'I do understand, though,' Sloan forged on, 'that this particular coat had recently been mended for your ninetieth birthday.'

'Yes, indeed, Inspector. It was quite restored for me. Wasn't that thoughtful?'

'Who by?' The sentimental side could wait.

'I think you might say it amounted to a conspiracy.'

'A conspiracy?'

'Shall we say then,' the Judge's lips twitched into something approaching a smile as he searched through his memory for the right phrase, 'by a number of the residents here acting in concert.'

'How?'

'Well, the Brigadier devised various ploys to keep me out of the grounds and therefore not needing my coat.' He chuckled. 'I only worked out afterwards how he had been diverting me whenever I showed signs of wanting to take a constitutional in cold weather.'

'And?'

'I am told that after Mrs McBeath had worked on it – she's the needlewoman here, you know – Captain Markyate wore it into Berebury and left it at the cleaners.'

'I see.' Detective Inspector Sloan noted that the Judge was able to mention Mrs McBeath's name without a quaver. 'And then?'

'Miss Ritchie – that's Walter Bryant's lady friend – collected it and delivered it back here under cover of darkness.' He looked rather wistfully at Sloan and said, 'She still drives, the lucky woman. And lucky Walter.'

'Quite,' said Sloan drily.

'Dowries come in all shapes and sizes these days,' said the Judge, 'only it's the car that's coming with the bride and not the other way round.'

'The coat . . .' said Sloan.

'Ah, yes,' he said urbanely. 'The coat. They presented it to me with a nosegay which Miss Bentley had made up. Judges, you know, used to be presented with a nosegay in olden times when they came to court to ward off infection. Gaol fever and so forth.'

'It's always been a risky job,' said Sloan. There had been something, in judicial history about the gift of a pair of white gloves, too, but he couldn't call the exact details to mind. Not at this moment.

'I thought it was very thoughtful of them,' said Gillespie. 'There's not a lot that you can give a man my age that he hasn't got already or doesn't want.'

What Sloan wanted were facts.

'Was there something hidden in the coat?' asked Detective Inspector Sloan, wondering if he was going to get a lecture on the asking of leading questions.

Calum Gillespie's lips twitched. 'A *diarium secretum*? No, Inspector. All I may have had there was a list of residents and former residents – oh, and my library list. Books,' he added blandly, 'are a great comfort when you get to this stage of life.'

'It would be very helpful at this stage, sir,' said Detective Inspector Sloan formally, 'to know if you have any enemies.' He hadn't got his notebook out yet but it was there, ready.

'All judges have enemies, Inspector,' he wheezed. A faint note of surprise came into his cracked voice. 'You should know that.'

'Any enemies at the Manor,' said Sloan steadily. One of the many wise things he had learned at his old Station Sergeant's knee had been the importance of not being frightened of judges.

'You mean they might be doing injury by proxy,' the old man mused, 'attacking my coat instead of sticking pins into a wax figure?' He stroked his chin. 'Now that is an interesting concept.'

'It doesn't answer my question, though, sir, does it?' Something else that that same wily old sergeant had drummed into him had been to be wary of anyone who responded to a question with a question of their own. Doctors did that a lot.

'Perhaps not,' the Judge sighed. 'Since the coat has absolutely no intrinsic value, Inspector, I must regretfully conclude that the choice lies between an outbreak of gesture politics or the damage being the work of a mind deranged.'

Sloan tried another tack. 'And which would you think the more likely?'

'Malice or madness? I've no idea at all, Inspector.'

'Perhaps, then, sir,' said Sloan, who himself was thinking along the lines of a more businesslike 'means, motive and opportunity', 'you might care to offer an opinion on why Mrs Morag McBeath has gone missing this morning.'

'God bless my soul!' he exclaimed, sitting bolt upright in his chair. 'Morag McBeath! But she isn't even ill.'

'The last person I should have expected to get lost,' said Captain Markyate, visibly stricken. 'Poor old Morag.'

Detective Constable Crosby had encountered the Captain on the drive in front of the Manor after

Markyate returned from his abortive search of the further part of the grounds. Markyate declared he had seen nothing and nobody out of doors save Hazel Finch, who had told him she was just slipping down to the village shop. She would ask there if anyone had seen Mrs McBeath.

'How come Mrs McBeath was the last person you'd have thought would go missing?' asked Crosby, who had yet to master some of the finer points of questioning a witness.

'She was one of the youngest residents here, Constable, that's why.' Somehow Markyate seemed more positive in the open air. 'And very fit for her age.'

Crosby frowned but kept silent. Political correctness had been added to the burdens of today's police officer and he wasn't at all sure where ageism came into all this.

'She didn't marry Charlie McBeath, you see, until well after the war,' explained Markyate.

Where the detective constable came from, so to speak, the younger the woman the more likely she was to have met a violent end, but he did not say so. Instead he said that he didn't see what her age had got to do with Mrs McBeath getting lost and did the Captain?

'No, no,' said Markyate hastily.

'What would you say, then, had got to do with it?' asked Crosby a trifle naively. He had been sent on his way to set up an incident room for a large-scale search. But all information was grist to a detective's mill: Detective Inspector Sloan, for one, was always saying so.

Captain Markyate stood uneasily on the gravel, shifting his weight first from one foot then to the other. 'Blessed if I know,' he said eventually, for once sounding almost animated. 'Someone's playing very dangerous games around here . . .'

'Dangerous games usually mean high stakes,' said Detective Constable Crosby feelingly, 'but not always.' It wasn't so very long ago that he had flatly refused to abseil down the cliffs at Kinnisport in aid of a police charity. That game was not worth a candle.

'And risk and reward are usually linked,' murmured Captain Markyate, adding almost to himself, 'except perhaps by the military authorities in times of war.'

'You saw action, sir?' asked Crosby, a little shyly. That, he knew, was what separated the men from the boys, and always had.

A grim little half-smile played round the Captain's lips. 'I don't think there's a man at the Manor who didn't, Constable. That's the whole trouble here.'

'And were you, sir,' asked Crosby, still unusually diffident, 'at that Tinchel or whatever they call it at Wadi el Gebra?'

Markyate nodded. 'Indeed, I was. It was very nasty. We were completely surrounded and under continuous fire. In fact, I still wake in the night and wonder . . . I dare say we all do.'

'Wonder what?'

'How we got out at all.'

Crosby suddenly remembered he was first and foremost a detective; a mind scarred might be a factor in an investigation. 'Do any of you here suffer from that post-traumatic stress syndrome that they're always talking about?'

'All of us who were there suffer from shell-shock,' said Markyate diffidently, 'but only some of us complain of it.'

'Who were there then and are here now?' asked Detective Constable Crosby.

'All the men,' said Markyate, 'and the widows of some of them.'

'Mrs McBeath?'

'No. Her husband was on the Staff.'

'Mrs Forbes?'

'Yes.'

'The new lady?'

'Mrs Carruthers? Yes. Her husband was there.' He closed his eyes, the better to read his memory. 'We'd been re-formed, you know. The second battalion had been practically wiped out at St Valéry.'

'Mrs Powell?'

'Her, too. Donald Tulloch had been gazetted to us just before we went into action.' Peter Markyate winced. 'It was a terrible baptism of fire. Terrible.'

Detective Constable Crosby, who had never experienced a shot fired in anger, searched for another phrase he'd once heard. 'And what about survivor guilt?'

Peter Markyate smiled tolerantly. 'Oh, yes, Constable, some of us suffer from that too.'

'If it was me,' said the constable simply, 'I would have been glad I'd survived.'

'I wonder if you would,' murmured Markyate. 'It might, you know, even be one of the places where your risk and reward come in.'

'We in the detective branch,' said Crosby grandly, 'call the motive the "reward" and we'll be looking for the reason why Mrs McBeath has taken off.'

'I'm sure you will,' agreed Markyate gravely. His tall asthenic figure seemed to be tiring now.

'And by the time we find her,' said Crosby with all the confidence of youth, 'I dare say we'll know all the answers. Now, tell me which parts of the grounds you've covered and where I'll find the Brigadier . . .'

'A what?' howled Superintendent Leeyes down the telephone line from distant Berebury.

'A dirk,' said Sloan. He couldn't see – but could sense – the Superintendent's rising choler. 'It's a sort of Scottish dagger with a long blade,' he added lamely. Leeyes must have finished the Saturday morning shopping run, because he had been at home when Sloan had rung him. Perhaps it was the possibility of missing his Sunday morning golf round that was upsetting him so much. He was a great one for complaining that he always got all of the kicks and none of the ha'pence, was the Superintendent.

'Sounds as unlucky as that Scottish play nobody's supposed to mention by name,' commented Leeyes.

'It's missing from the library,' Sloan informed him, 'here at the Manor.'

'Just like Mrs McBeath,' the Superintendent said ominously.

'I'm afraid so, sir.'

'A dirk doesn't sound like a very good book to me,' remarked Leeyes.

'More of a memento, I think, sir.' It had been hanging on the wall next to a curious relic with anthropomorphic overtones from the Ashanti Wars but Sloan didn't think it was necessary to mention this.

'Am I,' demanded the Superintendent rhetorically, 'now supposed to say "Hoots, mon", and make other Scottish noises?'

The only noises Detective Inspector Sloan, working policeman but also a live human being, had wanted to make were anxious ones about Mrs McBeath's present whereabouts.

And safety.

'You don't need me to remind you, Sloan,' said Leeyes, 'that stab wounds are always more dangerous than they look.'

'No, sir.' It was a lesson learned early and well on the beat but one always impossible to teach young men who were 'jealous in honour, sudden and quick in quarrel'. Sloan had long ago decided that each generation had to get its own feet wet in the matter of knives. 'What I'm afraid of, sir, is that whoever's got that old weapon knows all about stab wounds already.'

Leeyes grunted. 'Better check, then, that there's no one out and about who might have ideas of his own about what to do with strange Scottish knives.'

'Yes, sir.' Sloan would have been one of the first to admit that so-called 'Care in the Community' had added a new dimension to some police work. Their Assistant Chief Constable, very much the graduate police officer, always referred to that sort of care as *soi-disant* but Sloan had been too busy to find out why. 'The Matron here can't think of any reason why Mrs McBeath should have wandered off.'

'Talking of reasons, Sloan,' Leeyes said, 'have you come up with any to account for that other old party thinking she had been done to death yet?'

'Not yet, sir.' He was going to have to sit down soon and think about what could be considered worth the horrors of killing and being killed for. It wouldn't be easy. According to the poet the only things worth the labour of winning had been laughter and the love of friends. Half a lifetime in the police force had made Sloan doubt that as motives went laughter and the love of friends ranked very high on the scale but he could be wrong about that . . . he'd been a member of the constabulary long enough now to know that he could be wrong about anything. Or everything. Certainly about the death of a bedridden old person such as Mrs Gertie Powell. Or any old person . . .

Or any old person . . . A limerick learned long ago danced into Sloan's mind from the depths of his subconscious memory. 'There was an old person of Basing, whose presence of mind was amazing . . .' He pulled himself up with a jerk. 'I'm sorry, sir, I didn't quite catch what you were saying.'

'I said,' repeated Leeyes impatiently, 'that you'd better check on all the men at the Manor. You never can tell with "soldiers from the wars returning".'

'Very true, sir,' said Detective Inspector Sloan, placing the quotation without difficulty from last winter's evening course on 'The Poetry of War'. He decided against saying that you never could tell either with a missing old lady and an arcane – and absent – weapon.

It wasn't a combination he, for one, liked one little bit.

Chapter Seventeen

See where the victor-victim bleeds

Asked a question about the absent dirk the Matron wasn't able to be specific about the timing of when she had last seen it. This should have been a help. In fact, all it did was worry Detective Inspector Sloan even more.

'It wasn't there in the library this morning, Inspector,' she said. 'I'm sure about that.'

'When?'

'When I took Mr Bryant's two daughters along there,' she said. 'I went through with them both to the library myself because I was a little concerned that in their father's present condition an over-emotional visit from his daughters might overtax him.'

'What condition?'

'He's got a bad heart as well as the leg injuries he got in the war which put him in his wheelchair.'

'Ah.' If there was one thing which every policeman knew it was that families were bad for every medical condition, but especially for heart ones. Legs were less important.

'He told me he planned to tell his two daughters about his proposed remarriage over coffee in the library,' said Muriel Peden.

'Brave man,' commented Sloan.

'And that he'd also arranged for Miss Ritchie to join them all after he'd broken the good news to them.'

'Even braver,' observed Sloan.

A faint smile crossed Mrs Peden's face. 'He was brave enough at their famous Tinchel where he was wounded. The others have all told me so many, many times. So,' she added with an attempt at lightness, 'a domestic encounter shouldn't have held too many terrors for him.'

'Perhaps not.' In wartime, though, a man at least usually knew where the enemy lay. The placing of minefields and tank traps on the home front was never quite so straightforward. Sloan would have been the first to advise against any family meeting so very tightly structured. Asking for trouble, he would have said that was.

'But he did realize,' she admitted, 'that his daughters might not welcome the news.'

Sloan said he'd never met any adult daughter – married or single – who had ever welcomed the idea of her father's remarrying. Glad tidings they never were, however troublesome the old man was. 'I suppose,' he added doubtfully, 'that it's a sort of reverse Oedipus complex or something.'

'That's much too deep for me, Inspector,' the Matron responded firmly, 'but I am sorry that I can't remember when I last saw that dirk there. Yesterday, perhaps. Or the day before.' She smiled wanly. 'Yesterday was quite a day.'

Sloan said, 'Tell me about the dirk.'

'In its way, it was quite striking – for one thing, it was well over a foot long covered in a sort of basket-weave design and decorated with studs, to say nothing of the regimental crest.'

Sloan nodded. That was something a woman would have noticed. Especially a woman who did tapestry work.

'There would have been quite an empty space on the far wall had it not been there,' she insisted. 'I wouldn't have missed that.'

'It sounds quite a weapon . . .' said Sloan. The size and shape of the dirk – and, more significantly, its absence – were only some of the many things which were worrying him now.

'Well, it definitely wasn't there before his two daughters came,' she insisted. 'I didn't see the going of them myself. Nor, now I come to think of it,' she added, looking a little puzzled, 'have I seen Mr Bryant's Miss Ritchie arrive yet.'

Detective Inspector Sloan raised his head sharply at that. 'Then we'd better soon find out what has happened to her, too.'

Muriel Peden gave him a quick nod. 'I was told, Inspector, that she and Mr Bryant plan to get married quite soon.'

That, as far as Sloan was concerned, was something else for him to be worried about. He asked, 'Is there any connection between Mrs McBeath and Walter Bryant?'

She shook her head. 'Not that I know about. I understand Mrs McBeath didn't marry until after the war and she's definitely not one of those who go on about the past all the time.'

'Things not being as they used to be?' suggested Sloan.

' "Battles long ago",' murmured the Matron astringently, 'are what most of the men here usually dwell on, Inspector. Some don't, of course. The Brigadier never talks about the past and Captain Markyate hardly ever. The Judge talks a lot about it but never says anything, if you know what I mean.'

'And Mrs McBeath?'

She frowned. 'I'm pretty sure from what the others say that Mrs McBeath's husband wasn't involved in action very much.'

Something from his schooldays came into Sloan's mind, dredged up from a half-remembered lesson on war in ancient history. 'Go hang yourself, brave Crillon. We fought at Arques and you were not there.' 'So he didn't have anything to "remember with advantages"?' he said aloud, matching her sentiments. There were those, he knew, who were of the opinion that William Shakespeare had been a soldier. There were those, too, in plenty, who had things to remember with disadvantages – the sufferers from shell-shock, for a start. He'd have to ask Dr Browne about that.

'I think not,' the Matron said, 'But you should know, Inspector, that Mr Bryant has already informed us officially that he'll be leaving for good in under a month.'

That at least, thought Sloan, was another fact in a case singularly short of them.

'We shall miss him at the Manor after all the years he's been here,' she said.

'I'm sure. Now, what I must do first is see Mrs McBeath's room. But even before that, I want to know all about this coat of the Judge's in the cloakroom . . .'

Unfortunately in the matter of the timing of the damage to the Judge's coat the Matron was less able to be helpful. She hadn't been in that particular room herself since the morning of the day before, when she'd done a swift round to check that all was in order there before the funeral yesterday morning but not since.

Suddenly, thought Sloan, making yet another note, yesterday seemed a long time ago. 'Go on,' he said.

'As far as I can see, Inspector, anyone could have gone in there after that and before Miss Bentley discovered it in its damaged state this morning,' she said. 'Anyone at all.'

Sloan made another note. At this rate, his note-book would be full of information but still be without a single deduction, logical inference or conclusion in sight. And that wouldn't go down at all well with Superintendent Leeyes.

'And,' added Mrs Peden, 'whoever it was who did it could have slashed the coat there without anyone seeing them. They'd only have to lock the door and they'd have all the time in the world.'

'When was the Judge's birthday?' Sloan fortified himself with the thought that there must be fixed points in every criminal universe.

Muriel Peden's brow wrinkled. 'About three weeks ago.'

'So why,' said Sloan as much to himself as to the Matron, 'has it taken so long for someone to attack his coat?'

Detective Constable Crosby had never darkened 'Afric's burning shores', and so the similarities between seeking Brigadier Hamish MacIver and tracking a bull elephant on the rampage were quite lost upon him. They were, however, there; particu-larly in the leaving of a trail of broken branches and waving fronds of vegetation.

Crosby, like any other Great White Hunter, fol-lowed a route marked by flattened long grass and trampled twigs, eventually locating his quarry plunging about in the undergrowth surrounding the car park.

'Any news?' panted the Brigadier, stumbling back to the path in a state of great perturbation. 'Have you found her?'

'Not yet,' said Crosby.

The Brigadier, flushed and gently perspiring, adjusted his gammy leg to the hard ground. 'Who'd have thought it would be Mrs McBeath of all people who would go AWOL?'

Crosby looked quite blank. 'AWOL?' he echoed.

'Absent Without Leave,' barked the Brigadier. 'Didn't you know that?'

'No.' The only people in Crosby's book who went absent without leave were convicted prisoners or those on remand. Mrs McBeath hadn't even been arrested.

'Sorry,' MacIver grunted. 'I was forgetting you wouldn't be old enough to remember. By the time I was your age, my boy, I'd been in uniform for years.'

'So have I,' said Crosby, sounding injured. 'Only I'm plain clothes now.'

'What? What?' he said, and then, changing his tone, 'Oh, I see what you mean. Well,' he waved his arm over a wide sweep of landscape, 'I thought I'd better work my way systematically round this side of the house before going further out, fan-wise.' He squared his shoulder and recited a military maxim learned in the field long ago. 'You should always clear the foreground first.'

'Yes, sir, I'm sure.' It was the home ground that the police always cleared first. Escaped prisoners usually had, perforce, to head for home. Ten to one, there was nowhere else for them to go for shelter and support. Crosby couldn't begin to imagine where McBeath might have sought succour – if she had – since presumably she no longer had a home to go to.

'It's only after you've cleared the foreground,' went on the Brigadier, 'that you can safely advance.'

'We're waiting for reinforcements,' said Crosby, deciding that two could play the military metaphor game.

'The trouble with reinforcements,' said the older man bitterly, 'in my experience, is that they don't always come.'

Detective Constable Crosby was with him there. He himself had got his first black eye in the line of duty for trying to sort out a pub brawl while waiting for help to arrive.

'Or if they do come,' said the Brigadier, 'they arrive too late to do any good.'

'That's what happened to me, too,' said the constable simply. 'It was all over bar the shouting by the time help got to me.'

'It was all over bar nothing, I can tell you,' said the old soldier vigorously, 'by the time they got to Wadi el Gebra.' He narrowed a pair of rheumy eyes at the memory. 'Nothing except the sandflies, that is. They, like the poor, were always with us in the desert.'

'That where you got your limp?' asked Crosby.

'Tripped down some stairs at my club,' said the Brigadier shortly.

'That Mrs Chalmers-Hyde who died . . .' said Crosby suddenly.

'Maude?' said the Brigadier. 'What about her?'

'Was her old man in the war with you all?'

'Not exactly,' said the Brigadier, shaking his head. 'He was a bit too young at the time for that, but he was in the Army of Occupation after the war and then he was posted to the Control Commission. Why do you ask?'

'I just wondered,' said Detective Constable Crosby.

They were interrupted by the arrival at high speed of a small car whose driver took the turning into the car park at a thoroughly dangerous rate of knots before coming to a noisy halt immediately in front of the two men.

A younger, more active version of the genus elderly lady than the other women at the Manor stepped out and waved gaily to the Brigadier.

'Sorry to be late,' she called out. 'Wretched car just wouldn't start. Had to get a man to fix it. Walter and the girls will be wondering what on earth's become of me, won't they?' She turned in the direction of the Manor. 'Oh, look. There's Walter now, talking to someone on the drive. He must have been looking out for me. Isn't he a dear?'

The Brigadier grunted non-committally at this, while Detective Constable Crosby said nothing.

Miss Ritchie waved. 'Walter, this way . . .'

There was an answering wave from the figure in the wheelchair and the machine started off slowly in their direction, bumping over the gravel towards the waiting three. There was a distinct change in its pace, though, as it reached the top of the downward slope leading to the car park.

Miss Ritchie's expression of welcome and delight changed first to one of consternation and then to one of frank alarm as the wheelchair gathered speed. Gaining extra momentum at every yard, the little vehicle bounced forwards down the hill towards them.

'Brake, Walter, brake!' Miss Ritchie shouted. 'You're going too fast. Slow down or you'll crash!'

But braking, it seemed, was something that Walter Bryant could not do. Before the group's spellbound gaze, the wheelchair advanced upon their triumvirate at an ever-increasing rate.

Detective Constable Crosby was the first to come to life. Averting his fascinated stare from the speeding Walter Bryant, he pushed Miss Ritchie out of the line of the approaching machine and jumped himself just as it shot past him. As it rocketed by, its footrest caught the Brigadier just as, hampered by his gammy leg, that old soldier was trying to move to the safety of the bushes.

The next thing Detective Constable Crosby saw was the misshapen form of Walter Bryant describing an uncertain parabola, base over apex, into the bushes. And the Brigadier completely bowled over by a glancing blow from the side of the vehicle.

What the young policeman saw after that – and that only out of the corner of his eye – was the figure of a man hurrying away from the top of the drive.

Chapter Eighteen

Your heads must come
To the cold tomb

'I know, Sloan, that criminology is not considered by some academics to be one of the exact sciences,' Superintendent Leeyes sounded at his most peppery, 'but I should appreciate a more coherent account of precisely what is going on at the Manor at Almstone.'

Detective Inspector Sloan took a deep breath. 'And I should like to be in a position to be able to give it to you, sir.'

'Is it simply a case of one or more unfortunates going to their doom,' he asked nastily, 'or are things being done wholesale out there now?'

'That I can't say yet, sir. All I can say is that at least eight people have died at the Manor in the last three years.'

'And we know the doctor voiced his suspicions,' Leeyes reminded him, 'about one of those deaths.'

'Unconfirmed, though, by the pathologist at post-mortem,' countered Sloan.

'And,' said Leeyes, undeterred, 'another one who raised her own doubts. In writing.'

'Confirmed as baseless at post-mortem,' said Sloan steadily.

'And . . .?'

'And this morning two men were injured and one woman is missing.'

'That, Sloan, is precisely what I meant by wholesale.'

'Whether those injuries were sustained by accident or intent, sir,' Sloan ploughed on, 'we are not as yet in a position to say.'

Detective Constable Crosby wasn't actually in a position to say anything. He was in the kitchen of the Manor having his scratches attended to by the Matron. Walter Bryant and Hamish MacIver had been given tea and sympathy and now were resting in their rooms. Of Mrs Morag McBeath there was still no sign.

Walter Bryant was dazed and bruised and might or might not have sprained his right wrist. The Brigadier was both shaken and stirred but not apparently much injured. He had gone to his room under protest. What was significant was that Crosby had reported that neither man had said anything at all – to each other or to anyone else – after the accident.

'Not natural, sir, if you ask me,' he'd said.

'Early training,' divined Sloan.

Miss Ritchie had been – with some difficulty – dissuaded by Detective Inspector Sloan from following Walter Bryant to his room, on the grounds that she was in a position materially to assist the police with their enquiries.

That this was largely a matter of wishful thinking on Sloan's part only emerged after he had conversed with her.

Much more germane to the event had been a loose nut on the brake cable of Walter Bryant's wheelchair.

'Loose or loosened?' The Superintendent had swooped like the raptor he was.

'Somewhat less than finger tight,' said Sloan with impersonal accuracy. 'The forensic vehicle examiners are on their way out here now.' It was usually his friend Inspector Harpe of Traffic Division who sought their expertise, not him.

'I dare say, Sloan, that it's the first time they've been called out to an electric wheelchair.'

'Very probably, sir.' He paused. 'There are other complications, I'm afraid.'

'Well?'

'Just before the man in the wheelchair – Walter Bryant – set off down the path to the car park, Crosby thought he saw him talking to another man.'

'He either did or he didn't,' said Leeyes.

'He did,' capitulated Sloan. 'But he wasn't sure who it was at that distance.'

The Superintendent asked with elaborate patience whom Crosby had thought it had been then.

'Lionel Powell,' said Detective Inspector Sloan reluctantly.

'Well, well,' said Leeyes. 'The son of the most recently deceased of your cohort.'

'Yes, sir.' Sloan said carefully 'I have been told by the Matron here that he had been in touch with the Manor by telephone this morning in an attempt to recover the amulet ... ornament which had belonged to his late mother.' Sloan could almost hear his superior officer rubbing his hands together at this. He forged on. 'In the first instance, I am told, he had presented it to the Manor in her memory.'

'The son, eh . . .' Leeyes always preached that murder was first and foremost a family affair.

'Then today he discovered that his mother had indicated that she wished it given to someone else there.'

'Ha! Who?'

'Captain Peter Markyate.'

'It sounds to me, Sloan,' sniffed Leeyes, 'that what you should have had before you went out to that Manor is a thorough grounding in mid-fifteenth-century Italian politics.'

Detective Inspector Sloan had no difficulty in placing that sentiment. It came straight from an evening course that the Superintendent had once attended on 'Machiavelli – The Man and The Prince'. The study had been memorable in that it was one of the very few where the tutor and the Superintendent had both stayed the course. At the police station they had said it just demonstrated what they'd said all along: that Leeyes had a natural affinity with old Nick – and that the tutor had been a hero.

The thought of internecine complications immediately brought Sloan to something else: 'On the other hand, sir . . .'

'Yes?'

'One of the victims of this latest . . .' Sloan searched his mind for a word without overtones and, like many another public servant before him, settled on one that could mean anything at all ' . . . incident . . . had created potential problems with his two married daughters over his own remarriage.'

Leeyes pounced. 'Disinheritance?'

'Perhaps. Perhaps not.'

'Then find out, man.'

'Yes, sir.'

'That all, Sloan?'

Sloan hesitated. 'Nearly, sir.'

'Well?'

'After the – er – incident, Crosby found something lying on the ground just where the wheelchair had hit the Brigadier.'

'And did he recognize it this time?' enquired Superintendent Leeyes.

'Yes, sir.'

'The distance wasn't too much for him, then, I take it?' he asked sarcastically.

'No, sir.' Detective Inspector Sloan coughed. 'It

wasn't exactly difficult to identify either. It was the missing dirk.'

The Matron was prepared to swear to this being the weapon taken from the library. 'No doubt about it, Inspector.'

She had not, however, seen Lionel Powell at the Manor before or since the accident.

'Just look at that lovely carved handle, Inspector,' she said. 'It must be an antique.'

'Don't touch it,' adjured Sloan quickly. He himself held out little hope that there would be any finger-prints on the dirk, but he was determined that the detective decencies should be maintained in front of strangers – especially professional ones.

The Matron, her hands full of gauze and ban-dages, had showed no inclination to touch anything.

'Get a general call out for Lionel Powell, Crosby, as well as Morag McBeath,' Sloan instructed the con-stable wearily. 'He won't get far. And, Matron, can we have the names and addresses of Walter Bryant's two daughters?'

'Certainly, Inspector. I'll go and get them for you now.' She tied the last bandage neatly round Crosby's elbow, saying before she left the room, 'You're going to have a big bruise there tomorrow, Constable, I'm afraid.'

Detective Constable Crosby pulled out his pocket radio and then rested his injured elbow gingerly on the kitchen table. 'I'm hungry,' he said as soon as he had transmitted his message.

'The cook seems to have gone,' said Sloan. It was only one of the many disappointments crowding in on him now. 'She's not here, anyway.'

'What are we going to do then, sir? Toss for it?'

'For what?'

'Which one of those two old boys it was who had that knife.'

'Three.'

'Three?'

'You're forgetting the man on the terrace. He could have dropped it in the wheelchair.'

The constable leaned over and squinted at the dirk again. 'It doesn't looked as if it's been used lately but you never can tell.'

'No,' agreed Sloan. 'Not just by looking.' He was conscious of a great wish to find out more without invoking the specialists. Detection shouldn't be just a matter of assembling reports from other professionals, each expert only in their own field, none interested in the whole picture. Detection should, instead, be a question of studying the evidence and going on from there to reach a logical conclusion – and preferably the only possible correct conclusion at that.

And then proving it.

It didn't look as if this was going to happen in this case – if there was a case. He didn't even know that for certain yet. For all he knew, Gertrude Powell might have died from natural causes, just as Maude Chalmers-Hyde had been demonstrated to have done. Just as the doctors said she had . . .

'And we still don't know for sure who that dagger thing was meant for either, sir,' said Crosby insouciantly. 'Do we?'

'I think we might have an educated guess,' said Sloan absently, his mind elsewhere.

'The old girl who's gone missing?'

'I think she might have thought so,' murmured Sloan, 'which is what matters.' Now he came to think about it, none of the textbooks on the investigation of homicide that he had studied ever mentioned lunch. He decided that it was a serious omission.

'Presence of mind and absence of body,' said the constable. 'Can't beat it, can you, if it's safety you're looking for?'

'Thinking she was in danger is the best reason for her taking off,' agreed Sloan, 'although not the only one, of course.'

Detective Constable Crosby carefully adjusted his bad elbow on the table. 'If she is safe, that is.'

That was Detective Inspector Sloan's greatest worry. As far as he was concerned the first principle of first aid, 'Remove the patient from danger or the danger from the patient', applied to all police work, too. There was a quite different convention – and one which didn't apply to police work. He was beginning to wish now that it did. It was known as the 'Alan Smithie'. If a film director was given work on a second-rate production with which he did not wish his name – and therefore his loss of reputation – to be associated, he was allowed to use instead the dud name of Alan Smithie.

You couldn't do that in the Criminal Investigation Department of F Division of the Calleshire Force. There was no escape from an unlucky detective officer being associated with a dud case in the police. It hung round your neck like an albatross for ever.

'I'm hungry, sir,' said Crosby again.

'Then,' said Sloan crisply, 'you can start thinking about what worried Mrs McBeath so much that she decided to leave.'

'Probably the same thing that frightened Walter Bryant into wanting to marry and leave the Manor . . .' said Crosby.

They were interrupted by the return of Lisa Haines. She bustled in and went straight to one of the ovens. A tantalizing smell of chicken pie greeted the two men.

'Oh, good,' the cook said with relief. 'I was afraid it might have got over-cooked . . . feeding poor Mrs Forbes is such a slow business, but Hazel had to go down to the village for the Judge. Seeing as how she wasn't wanted any more to help look for the other poor lady . . .'

'Say that again,' said Sloan urgently.

'About poor Mrs Forbes? She's quite helpless and—'

'About Hazel,' thundered Sloan.

'The Judge asked her to take his torch down to the shop in the village.'

Detective Inspector Sloan was on his feet in an instant. 'Come along, Crosby. Let's get going . . . quickly.'

'But, sir,' protested the constable, 'the chicken pie . . .'

He was talking to thin air. In three quick strides Detective Inspector Sloan had left the kitchen and was on his way to the front door.

They overtook the care assistant walking along the road down to Almstone.

'Oh, Inspector, nothing else awful's happened has it?' Hazel Finch stopped in her tracks as soon as she saw the police car.

'Not yet,' said Sloan grimly.

'What's the matter then?'

'Nothing,' said Sloan. 'We'd just like a quick look at the Judge's torch.'

'He said it wasn't working, that's all,' said the bewildered girl. 'He wanted me to leave it at the shop to get some new batteries fitted.'

'Not quite all, I think,' said Sloan, taking it from her and unscrewing the barrel. He knocked out two batteries. Then he slid his fingers into the empty casing and eased out a small sheet of paper. 'I think this is what everyone's been looking for.'

Detective Constable Crosby so far forgot his bruised shoulder as to bend over to read what was written on the paper. He was patently disappointed at what he saw.

'It's just a list of the names of the people who've died here, sir,' he protested. 'That's all. And we've got a copy of them, anyway.'

'A list of only some of the names, Crosby,' pointed out Sloan gently. 'Not all of them.'

The detective constable took another look at the list and frowned. 'All right, then, sir. Six on here, eight on our list.'

'Can you remember who's missing?'

'Oh, I get you, sir.' He peered at the names. 'The two who aren't here, you mean?'

'I do,' said Sloan warmly.

Crosby screwed up his face in recollection. 'Mrs Kennedy and General Lionel MacFarlane,' he said eventually.

'That's right,' nodded Hazel Finch. 'Those two – they didn't die at the Manor. The General – he was knocked down by a van in Calleford last year, poor man. Killed outright.'

'And Mrs Kennedy?'

The girl furrowed her brow. 'She died in London after she had a fall up there. Ever so sad, it was. Gone up to her daughter's for Christmas, she had, and then that had to go and happen. A shame, wasn't it?'

Chapter Nineteen

Only the actions of the just

'So,' said Detective Inspector Sloan, 'someone . . .'

'The Judge,' said Crosby, his mouth full.

They were both ensconced in Matron's sitting room, each with a plate of chicken pie on his knee. Two men from the first panda car to reach the Manor – Constables Wilkins and Steele – were mounting guard over Walter Bryant and Hamish MacIver in their respective rooms, while the next pair of police to arrive were manning the front and back entrances to the Manor. Hazel Finch was presently giving an immobilized Walter Bryant and a bruised Brigadier their luncheons in the seclusion of their rooms.

'Probably the Judge, but still subject to proof,' said Sloan. The fact that the pace of the investigation had increased was more reason, not less, for being careful about jumping to hasty conclusions.

'All right, then, someone . . .' conceded Crosby, waving a fork in the air.

'Someone had carefully kept hidden a list of all the residents in the Manor who died there . . .'

'Except Mrs Powell,' pointed out Crosby. 'She wasn't on that list, was she, even though she snuffed it here?'

'Except Mrs Powell,' agreed Sloan, 'but not, remember, including those residents who happened to die away from the Manor.' This was the nub of the matter. He was sure of that now.

'Nothing criminal in keeping a list,' said Crosby obdurately.

'Nothing,' agreed Sloan.

'Nothing criminal, come to that, in someone else wanting to get their hands on a list,' the constable said. 'It's a free country.'

'A list that Mrs McBeath was afraid someone else would guess that she might have seen?' enquired Sloan ironically. 'So afraid that she's taken off . . .'

'Took her time to do it, though, didn't she?' Crosby chased a last piece of pastry round his plate with his fork. 'That's if she saw it when she did that repair job on the coat for the old geezer's birthday.'

'True,' agreed Sloan. 'So what's happened since then which might have changed things?'

'Gertrude Powell died, that's all,' said Crosby indistinctly. He finished the mouthful of chicken pie and went on, 'Oh, and that new woman arrived.'

'Mrs Maisie Carruthers,' said Sloan softly. 'I'd almost forgotten her.'

'She's been in her room all morning,' said Crosby. 'I checked like you said, sir. Her and her son.'

'Then sometime last night or very early this morning Mrs McBeath must have spotted the slashed coat in the cloakroom and put two and two together,' said Sloan. 'Which,' he added realistically, 'at the moment is rather more than we seem able to do, Crosby.'

'But,' said the constable profoundly, 'which two and two and which four?'

'That,' agreed Sloan, 'is the question.'

'We don't know who slashed the coat either,' said Crosby.

'Let alone why.'

'Our trouble, sir,' declared the constable with a sigh, 'is that we're seeing them as they all are now. They were probably younger when they got up to no good.'

'True,' conceded Sloan, veteran giver of evidence in juvenile courts. He didn't need telling that crime was age-related, that it was an activity that young males often grew out of. Though, unless he was much mistaken, malfeasance at the Manor would seem to disprove this.

Crosby laid his knife and fork carefully across his empty plate. 'Now that was really good.'

'And where do you go when you're an old lady with nowhere to go?' mused Detective Inspector Sloan, conscious that Mrs McBeath's safety ought to be his very highest priority now. To the naked eye, the blade of the dirk had seemed dry and clean but no true investigating officer could very well call that particular observation conclusive evidence that any weapon had never been used on a person in anger.

Not without Forensics saying so.

In writing.

'Social services?' suggested Crosby, worldly-wise in his generation.

'Church?' said Sloan, showing his age. Mrs McBeath was, after all, also of an age still to consider the church a source of succour. 'Or the hospital?' Even now, all such ports of call in Calleshire and every foot and motor patrol were being alerted. A cohort of reinforcements were already on their way from Berebury Police Station to join those on the spot in a search of the grounds of the Manor.

'Or is she with all the other runaways under the railway arches at Berebury?' asked Crosby with feeling. He didn't like what the drop-outs there shouted after him as he went past them. 'What I want to know, sir, is why that old judge made out that list of names in the first place.'

'He said it was so that he didn't forget old friends,' recounted Detective Inspector Sloan. 'How's that for a tale?'

'You don't need to write down six names to remember them,' said Crosby scornfully. 'Even if you are that ancient.'

'No,' agreed Sloan, 'you don't. So?'

'So?'

'So why did he do it?'

Crosby said, 'I can't think.'

Heroically resisting the temptation to comment on this naive admission, Sloan said mildly, 'It could just be, Crosby, that he had planned on that list of names being found after he'd died.'

Crosby considered this. 'Just like Mrs Powell wanted us to know what had been going on after she wasn't here?'

'So it would seem.'

'And someone else doesn't want us to,' said Crosby neatly.

'Keep going.'

'At least the Judge'd be safe then, wouldn't he, sir? If he was dead, I mean.'

'But safe from what?' asked Sloan, letting the theology of this slide by. 'I can't see that there could be anything left for him to be frightened of now.' At ninety, Sloan thought, surely one must be done with this world and things of this world – or was that wishful thinking?

'Conscience?' suggested Crosby slyly. 'That's, sir, if judges have consciences . . .'

'I doubt if it's that.' Sloan's latest encounter with Judge Calum Gillespie had been unfruitful to the point of pure exasperation. 'He's as bad as the rest of them. Wouldn't say a single word.'

'Closing ranks,' concluded Crosby, adding sedulously, 'Do you think there might be any more of that chicken pie left, sir, if I was to go back to the kitchen and ask?'

'Closing ranks against whom?' Sloan swept up the last mouthful on his own plate.

'Couldn't say, I'm sure, sir.'

'The Fearnshires versus the Rest?'

'For the honour of the Regiment, probably,' said Crosby, only well read in certain highly selective areas of British military history. He regarded his own clean plate with satisfaction. 'One thing, at least, the oldies don't have to worry about here is the food. It's good.'

'They would seem, though,' said Sloan acidly, 'to have plenty of other things to worry them. Like death, accidents and murder.'

'No wonder they have an Escape Committee,' said Detective Constable Crosby lightly.

'I'd forgotten about the Escape Committee,' admitted Sloan. That was just one more thing about the Manor that he hadn't really had time to go into yet. That wasn't meant as an excuse. It was only that in an ideal world, as one of his lecturers at the police training school always used to insist, good policemen should have all of the capabilities of the remontoir and he wasn't sure that he, Christopher Dennis Sloan, had half enough of them.

Then a young and keen Sloan, who had never even heard of the word, had waited for some other bright spark on the course to ask what it meant. He'd never forgotten the answer, delivered in the orotund tones of the lecturer – or its implications for an investigating officer.

'It's the mechanism,' the man had said so pompously, 'which regulates the power from the mainspring of a watch so that the force applied to the time-keeping element stays the same whether the instrument is nearly wound down or has just been wound up.' And he'd called them all 'officers of the watch' for the rest of the day to ram the lesson well and truly home.

As far as Sloan was concerned today, he – working police officer – was now very nearly wound down and he wasn't sure if his efficiency had stayed exactly the same as it had been when he had begun that morning.

'They'd need to get away from here once in a while, poor devils.' Crosby rose to his feet.

'They would, indeed.' There was an escape mechanism on a watch, too, he remembered.

'It's a proper God's waiting room, this place. I don't know about you, sir, but it gives me the willies.'

Time and tiredness, decided Sloan, were no excuse for detectives not following up each and every lead, even if the mainspring was running down. 'Yes, Crosby,' he admitted. 'I think I would want to get away once in a while, too, if I had landed here.'

'If I was put in the Manor, sir, I think I'd just pop my clogs straight away and have done with it,' said

Crosby insouciantly. 'Even if I wasn't completely gaga by then.'

'Easier said than done . . .' Sloan'd spoken casually enough but now he came to think about it . . . he pulled himself up with a jerk, something niggling at the back of his mind now.

'Me, I shouldn't just hang about waiting for that chap with the scythe . . .' persisted Crosby.

'The Grim Reaper.' Sloan made the connection without difficulty, his mind now suddenly switched to something Lisa Haines had said yesterday.

'I think I'll just nip along, sir, and see the cook,' said Crosby, plate in hand.

Sloan wasn't listening. He was trying to remember exactly what it was that that selfsame cook had said yesterday about poor Mrs Forbes. It hadn't seemed important at the time but there was an entirely different construction which could be put on that simple sentence about a dying woman: 'Of course,' Mrs Haines had said, 'she could die at any time. She does know that.'

He sat quietly, alone in the Matron's pretty little sitting room, thinking about the words and their two entirely opposite interpretations. Suppose any one at the Manor could die whenever they wanted to . . .

There was a word for that.

Euthanasia.

Or two words.

Easy death.

Not, at the Manor, physician-assisted euthanasia,

anyway, because Dr Angus Browne had refused to issue at least one death certificate – that for Maude Chalmers-Hyde.

That must mean something.

But what?

A hothouse of intrigue, that's what the Manor was, he decided. With undercurrents that he could feel but not see. And nobody here was going to tell him what they were. What was it that Crosby had said about closing ranks?

The door of the sitting room opened quietly but it was the Matron who came in. 'I've got the addresses of Walter Bryant's two daughters for you, Inspector.'

'Thank you.' That was something else that would need following up after Inspector Harpe's vehicle examiners had made their report on the brakes of Walter Bryant's wheelchair.

She hesitated. 'Is there any news?'

'Not yet,' he said. 'But there will be. Old ladies always turn up sooner or later. Tell me,' went on Sloan, since anything – anything at all – might be useful at this stage, 'what did Mrs McBeath's husband do in the war? Do you happen to know?'

'I gather he was on the Staff.' Muriel Peden gave a faint smile. 'I'm afraid the others didn't seem to hold the Staff in high esteem. I don't know why – but then I wasn't in the army in wartime.'

'Because it's usually behind the front line, I

expect,' said Sloan sapiently. 'I suppose that's where the Brigadier was, too.'

She frowned. 'I don't think so. He was at the Tinchel, I'm sure.'

A memory stirred in Sloan's mind. 'He wasn't mentioned in the history.'

'Really? Well, he was definitely there and,' she gave her faint smile again, 'I can tell you he's in great fighting form now. Hazel's got him into bed at last but it wasn't easy. He won't say anything except that he wants to know where to find Lionel Powell.'

'He's not the only one,' said Sloan astringently. 'We're still looking, too . . . Tell me, Matron, which is Mrs Carruthers' room?'

'Police.' Inspector Sloan introduced himself without preamble.

Mrs Carruthers was in bed, her son still reporting on what he could see from the window.

Ned Carruthers, for whom the police force had vague subconscious associations with the attacking of protesters trying to protect the environment, immediately went on the defensive. 'You must remember that my mother's an old woman, Inspector,' he said. 'She shouldn't be disturbed like this . . .'

Mrs Carruthers sat up, eyes bright with excitement. 'What's happened now?'

Ned was undeflected in his protection of his

mother. 'After all, she only arrived at the Manor two days ago. She can't possibly be of any help to you with your enquiries.'

Maisie cut off this display of filial piety by saying briskly, 'What is it you want to know, Inspector?'

'I understand, madam, that you've known some of the residents here for a long time.'

'A very long time,' she said with emphasis. She gave a mirthless laugh and added, 'Man and boy, you might say.'

'Including the late Mrs Powell?'

'A great girl,' said Maisie reminiscently. 'A great girl.'

'Did you know her in Egypt?'

Mrs Carruthers nodded vigorously. 'I'll say!'

Detective Inspector Sloan said, 'After her first husband was killed?'

'Yes.'

'Did you know her second husband?'

'Oh, yes.' She gave a high cackle. 'That marriage didn't last. Never thought it would.'

'Why not?'

'He didn't have what it takes,' said the old lady succinctly.

'Mother!' Ned Carruthers began another outraged protest.

She sniffed. 'Never had. Never will.'

Detective Inspector Sloan gave the figure in the bed a long considered stare. 'And are you going to tell me who he was or are you going to leave us to find out for ourselves?'

'Inspector,' began Ned Carruthers, 'I call this . . .'

Maisie gave Sloan a wickedly coquettish look. 'You'll get to know anyway, won't you?'

'It'll take longer, that's all,' said Sloan equably, 'and time may be something we don't have now.'

She turned her head away as if she was staring into the past and seeing the action all over again like an old film.

'Captain Markyate,' she said after a long pause. 'Peter Bertram Markyate.'

It was Ned Carruthers who spoke next, 'Everybody's uncle . . .'

Chapter Twenty

Smell sweet and blossom in their dust

'More, young man?' In the kitchen Lisa Haines bridled at Detective Constable Crosby and his empty plate with a mixture of pleasure and high indignation. 'After that great helping I gave you?'

'It was very good.'

'Who do you think you are? Oliver Twist?'

'The Thin Man,' said Crosby.

The cook looked him up and down. 'You could have fooled me.'

'Ah,' rejoined Crosby swiftly, 'but you can't fool me. That pie was the best I've had in years.'

'Don't you think you can sweet-talk me, Constable, and get away with it.'

'And the gravy was out of this world.'

'Flattery won't get you anywhere, either.'

Crosby lifted his head. 'Even the Inspector said so. He thinks your sauce is wonderful. Gravy raised to a higher power, he called it.'

'What do you mean?' she demanded with surprising belligerence. 'Even the Inspector!'

'He's a very critical man,' said Crosby earnestly.

'Hard to please, is he?' said the cook, opening the door of one of her ovens.

'Discriminating, Mrs Haines, that's what he is,' said Crosby, peering over her shoulder and inhaling a deeply satisfying aroma.

'More than can be said for some folks round here,' sniffed Mrs Haines.

'No pleasing the residents?' suggested Crosby, one eye on the pie dish. There were still a few segments of feathery pastry crust to be seen, each exuding a rich brown substance.

'If it isn't their teeth,' lamented the cook, 'then it's liver or stomach troubles. Terrible shame to get to their age and not to be able to enjoy your food, isn't it?'

The constable nodded. 'Terrible.'

'What's terrible now?' asked Hazel Finch, coming through the kitchen door with an empty tray in her hands. 'Have they gone and found Mrs McBeath?'

'Not being able to enjoy your food,' said Lisa Haines, who had her own culinary-based priorities. 'That's what's terrible.'

'It's not the only thing you can't enjoy when you're old,' said the care assistant vigorously. 'There's other things as well. Take Mr Bryant now . . .'

'He can't walk,' said Lisa Haines, giving the pie dish a considering look.

'And Captain Markyate can't ever make up his mind,' said Hazel Finch.

'Mrs Forbes,' said Crosby suddenly, 'she can't die.'

'She could,' said Lisa Haines, 'but she won't. That's her trouble.'

'And then there's Miss Bentley, who won't let go of being in charge . . .' said Hazel ruefully. 'Can't stop telling me what to do.'

'Comes of always being top, I suppose,' said Lisa Haines. She turned to Crosby. 'Here, Constable, give me your plate. I think I might be able to manage a second helping for you after all.'

Detective Inspector Sloan walked down the long corridor to the library and pushed open the heavy old door. Dust motes danced in the early afternoon sunlight which was streaming through the windows and somewhere a fly buzzed, but otherwise all was still.

'Matron told me I would find you here, Captain Markyate,' he said, pulling up a leather chair beside the old Fearnshire soldier. 'Might I join you? We'd like a word.' This wasn't strictly true since Crosby was nowhere to be seen but the police plural would suffice.

Markyate lifted his head politely. 'Please do. We're both here.'

Sloan spun round. 'Both?'

Markyate pointed. Sunk deep into a large armchair across the room was Lionel Powell. The civil servant raised his hand in Sloan's direction by way of acknowledgement but did not speak.

Sloan could have kicked himself. Pure Kipling, it was, Lionel Powell being in the library. Just like Captain Wentworth in 'Jane's Marriage' – 'in a private limbo, where none had thought to look.' Lionel Powell wasn't 'reading of a book', though. He was sitting attentively with Peter Markyate.

'There is a time,' said Detective Inspector Sloan portentously, conscious that he might almost have been reading aloud something from the Book of Ecclesiastes, 'for the truth to be told.' He cleared his throat and added a sentence that was quite his own, 'And for it to be known exactly who knows what.'

It was Lionel Powell who spoke. 'I now know, Inspector, why my mother wanted Captain Markyate to have that old Egyptian ornament.'

'My wedding present to her,' said Markyate, looking more like an attenuated strand of willow than ever. By contrast, Lionel Powell looked a new man.

'I picked it up in the souk,' said Markyate, 'the day we got married. I hadn't got a bean in those days. Not a bean . . .'

'That was the Tulloch treasure we were always hearing about,' said Lionel Powell calmly. 'My mother was forever talking about that.'

'It's what Gertie always called it,' said Markyate, 'to throw people off the scent.'

'You couldn't believe a word she said,' Lionel

declared fervently, accepting Markyate's statement without demur. 'Ever.'

'The scent of what?' enquired Sloan, although he thought he could guess by now.

'Our marriage,' Markyate said.

'Why,' asked Detective Inspector Sloan, 'should she want to do that?'

Captain Markyate lifted his head and said pallidly, 'It was not what Gertie called a proper marriage.'

'You went through a form of wedding ceremony,' said Sloan, consulting his notebook for what Maisie Carruthers had told him, 'in Alexandria in Egypt on . . .'

'Oh, the ceremony was all according to Cocker,' said Markyate readily. 'Nothing wrong with that.'

'So?' said Sloan, conscious that as Markyate spoke Lionel Powell was strangely relaxed.

'Any man can stand up and say "I will",' said the Captain, stirred almost to animation. 'But . . .' his light, high voice trailed away.

'But . . .' prompted Sloan gently. There were some things almost too difficult to put into words, and he suspected this was one of them.

'But as for the rest . . .' He opened his hands in a gesture of despair.

Lionel Powell demonstrated beyond all reasonable doubt that he was Gertie's son by asking with tactless clarity, 'Captain Markyate, are you trying to tell us that the marriage was not consummated?'

'Gertie was a great girl, always,' Markyate said obliquely, 'but I'm afraid I wasn't ever – er – a great chap.'

'And,' amplified Powell unnecessarily, 'that means, of course, Inspector, that there were no children of the marriage.'

'So . . .' invited Sloan.

'So we were divorced,' said Peter Markyate simply. 'And then Gertie married Hubert Powell.'

'That's a relief, I must say,' said Lionel Powell, a touch of acid in his voice. 'But why all the secrecy? That's what I don't understand.'

'Hubert's family would never have let him marry a divorcee. Not in those days. It was all a long time ago, remember, and they were always a stuffy lot, the Powells. A very long time ago,' he added, staring into the distance as if he could see the past before his eyes, just as Maisie Carruthers had done.

'Could they have stopped him?' came back Powell swiftly. 'Presumably he was of age.'

'Hubert's father held the purse strings,' said the Captain. He gave Lionel Powell a diffident smile. 'It was a very large purse and Gertie liked the good life, remember.'

Lionel Powell jerked his shoulders in grudging agreement of this. 'Naturally that is a factor for which my wife and I have always had cause to be grateful.'

Detective Inspector Sloan's mind was concentrating on something quite different.

'The late Mrs Powell's letters, gentlemen,' he said, 'which would seem to have been taken from her bedroom soon after her death . . .'

'They were,' said Peter Markyate. 'But not by me. They weren't there.'

'You went into her room for them?'

'I went there to try to retrieve my letters to her,' he said. 'Better not seen, you know.'

'That figures,' said Sloan.

'But they'd already gone, Inspector.' He shrugged his shoulders. 'I'd been beaten to it but by whom and why I can't tell you.'

'And the amulet?'

'I cleaned my fingerprints off that.' He gave them both a shy smile. 'I always patted it when I went in to see Gertie. For old times' sake, you know. And it made her laugh.'

Sloan stood up. There must be rhyme and reason to all this if he could just put his finger on it. He turned to Lionel Powell. 'And you, sir, were seen with Walter Bryant when his wheelchair took off down the drive.'

'That's right, Inspector,' said Powell at once. 'I gave him a push.'

'Why?'

Powell looked pained. 'Because he asked me to, of course. He thought he'd get there quicker with a good shove.'

'Walter spotted the missing dirk while he was in

here with his daughters,' explained Markyate, 'and we both went looking for Hamish.'

Detective Inspector Sloan stared at him, light beginning to dawn at long last. 'Tell me, what did the Brigadier do at Wadi el Gebra?'

The library was suddenly very quiet again except for the fly that was still buzzing at the window.

'He ran away,' said Markyate simply.

'But . . .' began Sloan, who thought wartime deserters were shot. At dawn. Not at eight o'clock. Eight o'clock had given time for a reprieve to reach a place of civil execution. There was no reprieve from a firing squad.

Markyate intruded on Sloan's private thoughts. 'But Walter and I caught him and brought him back.'

'To fight another day?'

'He did very well in Italy,' said Markyate. 'Made up for it there, all right, and later on in Normandy.'

'So nobody knew?'

'Not outside the Regiment,' said Markyate.

'Sir . . .' Crosby came after Sloan down the corridor, a plate of chicken pie balanced precariously in one hand. 'I think something funny's been going on here for a long, long time.'

'So do I,' said Sloan grimly.

'Something secret . . .'

'Too many things are secret here. That's the

whole trouble.' Sloan didn't slacken his pace. 'Which one do you have in mind, Crosby?'

'All those deaths here. And then there's Mrs Forbes. She's the old woman who won't die even though she could easily.'

'Easily could,' Sloan corrected him, 'is the name of that game. Put that plate down and follow me.'

The room that he made for was on the first floor and belonged to Brigadier Hamish MacIver. The old officer was lying on his bed rather than in it, Constable Wilkins on bedwatch beside him.

'It is time we had a talk, Brigadier,' said Sloan.

'Nothing to say,' growled MacIver.

'About the work of the Escape Committee.'

'Nothing to say,' he repeated.

'I think,' said Sloan, 'that here at the Manor your Escape Committee helped the incurably ill and old to die if they wanted to.'

The Brigadier said nothing.

'And you instituted something called the Pragmatic Sanction whereby residents gave the Escape Committee their blessing for being helped out of this world as and when their infirmities got too much for them.'

'Vets,' remarked the Brigadier offhandedly, 'do it all the time.'

'True. But it is not yet legal here and therefore naturally Judge Gillespie did not approve of it.'

'He's always been an old stick-in-the-mud.'

'The Judge kept a list of those residents whom

he suspected of having been killed in this manner in his old coat . . .'

The Brigadier sat up suddenly. 'He did what?'

'Mrs Powell,' said Sloan, 'was afraid that she might be killed in that way, too, and, as a noted lover of life, she, too, disapproved of the practice. She tried to draw attention to it after she was safely dead.'

'From beyond the grave,' said Crosby. 'Except that she didn't get there . . .'

MacIver wasn't listening. 'What did you say was in the Judge's coat?'

'A list of all those who had died here – except Mrs Powell.'

He sank back on his pillows, a little smile playing on his lips. 'Really?'

'You went looking for what you thought was in that coat on Friday evening.'

The Brigadier jerked his head up.

'Which was,' said Sloan inexorably, 'the same thing that you thought the late Mrs Powell might have kept among her letters, which you stole . . .' The Brigadier moistened his lips. 'An account of your attempt at desertion in the face of enemy fire at the Tinchel.'

The Brigadier's lips might have been dry but his old eyes were becoming suspiciously rheumy.

'But when Mrs McBeath saw that someone had slashed the Judge's coat,' said Sloan, 'she naturally assumed that someone had found that list and might very well try to kill her, too, since she would be presumed to have come across it when mending the coat, as indeed she probably had.'

'Very unlikely, I should have thought,' the Brigadier said, apparently unconcerned at this hypothesis.

'Unless she saw that the dirk had been taken from the library and took fright about that instead,' said Detective Constable Crosby.

'A possibility, of course,' said MacIver.

'And so for the second time,' said Sloan in a steely voice, 'one of your brother officers – Walter Bryant – had to save you from yourself. He noticed that the dirk had gone missing and guessed you'd gone hunting Mrs McBeath in case she'd found out about your dereliction of duty.' Sloan paused, a steelier note coming into his voice. 'I think Mrs Carruthers had her fears, too.'

Hamish MacIver raised his head at this.

'She knew about Wadi el Gebra – as did the wives of all the officers serving there. And she wondered – like Gertie – if you were intent on making away with everyone who had known about your defection under the guise of euthanasia.'

His head sunk slowly downwards between his hands. 'I knew she knew and she knew I did . . .'

'That's why she couldn't understand about Mrs McBeath being in danger.'

'McBeath was the Staff,' said the Brigadier thickly. 'Never saw action.'

'But Gertie's husband at the time wasn't. He was there and she knew, too.' In Sloan's considered view 'the bubble reputation' had a lot to answer for. 'But Mrs Chalmers-Hyde didn't. Her natural death fooled Dr Browne and allayed his suspicions.'

MacIver didn't seem to be listening any more.

That didn't stop Sloan from going on. 'When Walter Bryant saw you, he got Lionel Powell to speed him downhill towards you to stop you doing any-thing misguided with that dirk . . .'

The Brigadier seemed to be beyond speech.

'Lionel didn't know what it was all about and being a good civil servant simply removed himself from the scene of the action with all possible speed.' Detective Inspector Sloan, investigating officer, didn't go on. There was no need now. There was only a broken man to talk to.

'What did you say describes the situation best, Sloan?' snapped Superintendent Leeyes down the telephone. 'Never heard of it.'

'A double helix,' said Detective Inspector Sloan, forbearing to remind the superintendent about the instruction on DNA testing that they'd all had in the Force.

Leeyes grunted.

'But,' hastened on Detective Inspector Sloan, back in Matron's sitting room now, 'I think that the real trouble was that the Brigadier imagined it was something quite different that the Judge was keeping hidden and he acted accordingly.'

'Wheels within wheels is what you call that,' said Leeyes. 'Not all that fancy stuff about DNA.'

'He must have thought instead that the Judge had written down for posterity a full account of the action at Wadi el Gebra.'

Sloan took an instant policy decision against saying anything about 'the cannon's mouth'. He doubted if his superior officer was sufficiently familiar with Shakespeare's 'Seven Ages of Man'.

'About which you say there was this schoolboy conspiracy of silence,' barked Leeyes.

'Moreover, sir,' went on Sloan steadily, 'he also feared that the deceased – Gertie Powell . . .'

'I thought we were losing sight of her in all this, Sloan.'

' . . . might have had something about his desertion in her letters so he took those from her room after she'd died. Her first husband had been at the action there, too, you see.'

Leeyes grunted.

'I understand, sir, that Mrs Powell, even though she was very ill, had made it abundantly clear that she hadn't wanted any part in their Escape Committee's Pragmatic Sanction.'

'And did that save any of 'em from being done away with?' Superintendent Leeyes arrived unerringly at the kernel of the argument with his customary precision.

'I don't know how we can possibly tell at this stage, sir.' He cleared his throat and said, 'It isn't so much a case of time being of the essence as timing. They were all dying anyway.'

Leeyes grunted again. 'Surmise, most of it, Sloan.'

'Yes, sir,' admitted Sloan. 'We don't actually have much in the way of evidence.'

'Is that good or bad?'

Detective Inspector Sloan, police officer, said, 'That is not for me to say, sir.'

'The law,' said one of its professional upholders, 'is an ass.'

'Yes, sir,' said Christopher Dennis Sloan, man.

It was a little later when the telephone in Matron's sitting room rang again. Detective Inspector Sloan reached over to pick up the receiver. It was Dr Angus Browne.

'That you, Inspector? Good. I'm ringing from Larking. I've got one of my patients at the Manor here in my consulting rooms. She says she's run away from there. A Mrs Morag McBeath. What's that you say? No, she's not injured but she's a bit tired and shaky and she's babbling about being in danger from someone unspecified.'

'Not any more she isn't, doctor,' said Sloan vigorously. 'You can tell her from me that she's got nothing to worry about any more. Nothing. She can come back now. The Manor's quite safe again now.'